Short &
Shorter
Stories

Short & Shorter Stories

AMRITA BHARATI

JAICO PUBLISHING HOUSE

Ahmedabad Bangalore Bhopal Bhubaneswar Chennai
Delhi Hyderabad Kolkata Lucknow Mumbai

Published by Jaico Publishing House
A-2 Jash Chambers, 7-A Sir Phirozshah Mehta Road
Fort, Mumbai - 400 001
jaicopub@jaicobooks.com
www.jaicobooks.com

© Amrita Bharati, Bharatiya Vidya Bhavan

SHORT & SHORTER STORIES
ISBN 978-81-8495-750-1

First Jaico Impression: 2015

Page design and layout: R. Ajith Kumar, Delhi

Printed by

Contents

Folktales from Near and Far

Tales That Inspire

Tales of Wit and Wisdom

Folktales from Near and Far

The Red Silk Cotton

– A Folktale from Odisha

The red silk cotton is a tall tree that, flowers between January and March. It is found all over the sub-continent, including Sri Lanka and Myanmar. The trunk of the young tree has hard conical thorns that disappear, as the tree advances in age. Some people pull out the thorns to chew them.

An Odia tribal legend has a quaint explanation for the occurrence of the thorns.

The King of Judagarh had several wives, but all of them were sickly. So one day, he announced that he would give a big reward to anyone who could cure them of their illness.

A demon named Kaliya Dano, who had disguised himself as a sadhu, sent word to the king that he could cure his wives, but that they would have to come to his hut.

The unsuspecting king sent his wives to the sadhu, who ate them all.

The king soon learnt that he had sent his wives to a demon and came to battle with him.

On seeing him, the demon rushed up a red silk cotton tree. While ascending, he pulled out his teeth, one by one, and stuck them in the tree. The king, climbing up after him, could not get past the long, sharp teeth embedded in the trunk and finally gave up the chase.

He posted guards at the foot of the tree and left.

Kaliya Dano never came down from the tree, but ever since the encounter between him and the King of Judagarh, the red silk cotton trees have had thorny trunks.

Death Comes Calling

– Retold from *One Thousand and One Nights*

Mansur Ali's servant, who had gone to the market came running back and fell at his master's feet.

"What's the matter?" asked Mansur Ali.

"I… I have seen Death!" said his servant, his eyes rolling in terror. "I was buying fruits, when I felt someone's eyes on me. I turned around and… there he was… Death! Please give me a horse, master. I want to put as much distance as I can between him and me… I'll go to Baghdad and stay there for a few days."

Mansur Ali gave him his fastest horse and the servant rode away at breakneck speed. When he had gone, Mansur Ali decided to verify his story. He went to the market and began to wander among the stalls there and then, suddenly, he saw the fearful figure of Death coming towards him.

Mansur Ali was terrified, but he stood his ground. When Death drew near, he said to him, "Why did you frighten my servant?"

"Did I frighten him?" rasped Death. "I didn't mean to. It's only that I was surprised to see him here."

"Surprised? Why?"

"Because," said Death, grinning demoniacally, "I'm supposed to collect him at Baghdad tonight!"

The Snake That Reformed

– **A Folktale first told by Sri Ramakrishna Paramhansa**

A snake had bitten several people and the villagers were afraid to go near the field in which it resided.

One day, a scholar was passing by when the snake came slithering out of its hole, hissing loudly. The man however showed no fear and he had such a gentle look on his face so that the snake felt uneasy and slightly ashamed of itself.

"Why do you behave so badly?" asked the man and gently chided the snake for its wicked ways. The snake, abashed, writhed in embarrassment and promised not to bite anyone again.

It kept its word.

The villagers were at first surprised to see the snake behaving in such a docile manner, but once they got used to its new personality, they lost all fear of it. They began to pelt it with stones and drag it around by its tail.

One evening, the snake crawled to the scholar's house and complained bitterly about the way the people were treating it.

The scholar was moved to pity. "The people have lost their fear of you," said the man, "you should not have stopped frightening them."

"But it was you who told me to practice non-violence," protested the snake.

"I told you to stop biting," said the scholar quietly, "not to stop hissing."

Lessons in Thrift

– A Folktale from Europe

A man who prided himself on his thriftiness was dismayed to learn that, there was another tightwad, who lived more frugally than him.

"I must take lessons in thrift from this genius," he said to his son, "otherwise I'll continue to overspend. Go to his house and ask him if he will accept me as his student!"

It was customary to gift a goose to the guru, at the time he was approached. The would-be *chela* drew a goose on a piece of paper and gave it to his son.

"Give this to him with my regards," he beamed.

The boy set off, thrilled by his father's ingenuity. A true son of his father, the thought of giving away one of their geese had filled him with horror.

It took him half a day to arrive at his destination. The man he had come to meet was not at home, but his wife was there and she assured him that her husband would accept his father as his student.

The boy dutifully handed over the drawing of the goose to her. She took it and carefully placed it in a drawer.

It was customary for the teacher to acknowledge the gift with a lesser gift of his own.

"Please take these oranges for your father," she said, and went through the motions of handing over four oranges to him, picking them up one-by-one from the table beside her. Only, there were no oranges there at all.

Her husband returned shortly after the boy had left. She told him about the boy's visit, and the exchange of gifts.

"Good, good," said her husband. "We must not forget the social graces. But show me how you held the oranges."

When she showed him how she had held the imaginary oranges, her husband's brow darkened in anger.

"Oh, you wasteful woman!" he shrieked. "Did you have to hold your fingers so far apart?! Do you think we are millionaires that we can give away such BIG oranges!"

Not True

– A Folktale from China

M r. Kitchom loved to listen to stories, but at the end of the tale, he would invariably exclaim, "That can't be true!"

One day, he was standing at the gate of his house, when he saw the village schoolmaster going by. He called out to him and begged him to tell him a story.

"On one condition," said the teacher. "When I finish, you should not say, 'that can't be true.' If you say that, I'll be entitled to a sack of grain from your house."

"Agreed," said Mr. Kitchom.

"I'll tell you the story of a great lord, who lived in China a long time ago," said the teacher. "One day, this aristocrat got into his palanquin to go to the governor's palace. On the way, he heard a bird crying 'preeep... preeeeep.' When he peered out, the bird soiled his robe with its droppings.

The lord sent his servant back for a new robe and when he had brought it, he took off the soiled robe, threw it away and put on the new one. Then they resumed the journey. A little later, the bird called out again and when the lord peered out, it soiled his sword with its droppings. The nobleman sent his servant back for a new sword and when he had brought it, he gave the soiled one to the servant and kept the new one.

The lord made up his mind not to look out, if the bird cried out again, but when it did he could not resist looking out and this time, the bird dropped its load directly on his head.

The lord sent his servant to bring him a new head and when he had brought it, cut off his own with his sword..."

"Oh, but that can't be true!" blurted Mr. Kitchom.

"No, it can't," agreed the teacher, triumphantly, "but you've uttered the prohibited phrase and you agreed to forfeit a sack of rice as penalty!"

"Did I?" said Mr. Kitchom, slyly. "That can't be true."

Delivered to the Owner

— A Folktale from Vietnam

An old couple, struggling to keep body and soul together, decided to grow vegetables, on a patch of land, close to their house.

While they were digging up the soil, the old man's spade hit a wooden chest. When they opened the chest, they found it was full of gold coins.

"We're rich!" said the old woman, her eyes lighting up. "God has sent us help in the twilight of our lives!"

"We can't be sure of that," said the old man. "This land does not belong to us, so how can we say the gold is ours? Let it lie here, and if it is really meant for us, God will find a way to reach it to us."

So they re-buried the chest, and went away.

The old woman told everyone about their find, but no one was prepared to believe that she and her husband had walked away from a treasure. They felt that she was making up the story.

Now there lived in the village a grocer who yearned for wealth. He was sceptical about the old woman's claim, but one

night, it occurred to him that she had no reason to make up such a story. He decided to investigate.

He took his two sons along. They dug around a bit and found the chest. When they had hauled it out, the grocer, his hands trembling with excitement, threw back the lid.

A fearsome black snake reared its head, and it would have slithered out, if one of the grocer's sons had not quickly slammed down the lid.

"There's no gold here, only Death!" shrieked the grocer. "I'll teach that wily, old woman a lesson!"

He and his sons tied a rope around the chest, and dragging it to the old couple's house, left it outside their door. When the couple found it the next morning, they were overjoyed. There was a hole in the side of the chest, so perhaps the snake had left through it, because when they opened the chest there was only the gold for them to see.

"Now it is certain God wants us to have this gold," said the old man, carrying the chest inside, "otherwise he wouldn't have had it delivered to our house."

The two of them lived in ease and comfort for the rest of their lives.

How Two Bachelors Found Wives

– A Folktale from Africa

Tembo and Kalameleme were the only two bachelors in the village of Oba, in Central Africa. Both were warriors, but Tembo was gentle and had a helpful disposition, whereas Kalameleme was rude and rough; he was never known to help others out of kindness.

Early one wintry morning, Tembo was out hunting when he stumbled upon Moma, the great rock python. Tembo quickly put an arrow to his bow, and was about to shoot when Moma spoke.

"The cold has numbed me," said the python. "Take me somewhere, where it is warm so that I might regain my strength."

The warrior gathered the heavy reptile into his arms and tottering to a pool fed by hot springs, gently lowered the snake into the water. When Moma regained his strength, he thanked Tembo for saving his life, and asked him what he could do for him in return.

"Give me a bride, if you can," pleaded Tembo.

The reptile dived to the bottom of the pool, and returned with a pumpkin, which he presented to the warrior.

"Your loneliness will soon end," he promised.

When Tembo reached his village, the pumpkin fell from his hands, and began to grow in size. It became huge.

Finally, it broke, and a young woman stepped out from it.

"Who are you?" gasped Tembo.

"Your wife," smiled the woman.

So Tembo married. His bride had all the qualities he had hoped for; she was loving, caring, and like him, fond of good food. Tembo had never been happier in his life.

Now there was only one bachelor left in the village, Kalameleme. Everybody knew how Tembo had got his bride. Kalameleme decided to get a bride in the same way. One hot day, he went in search of Moma and eventually found him stretched out in the middle of the road, gasping for breath. Kalameleme put an arrow to his bow and raised it as if to shoot.

Finally, Moma spoke.

"The heat has sapped my energy," he said. "I can barely move. Take me to a cool spot, where I could regain my strength or I will surely die."

No sooner had the words left his mouth, than Kalameleme caught him by his tail and dragged him to a river. The snake was badly bruised, but Kalameleme did not care. He flung the reptile into the water.

When the python had regained his strength, he asked the warrior how he could reward him for saving his life.

"Give me a bride!" demanded Kalameleme.

The python dived to the bottom of the river and came up with a pumpkin that he handed over to Kalameleme.

"Your loneliness will soon end," he promised.

As Kalameleme was rushing home excitedly with the pumpkin, it fell from his hands, and began to grow in size. It became huge.

Finally it broke, and a giantess stepped out.

"Who are you?" gasped Kalameleme.

"Your wife," smiled the woman.

"No, no, I don't want a wife!" yelled Kalameleme, and turned to run.

But the giantess caught him by his leg and dragged him all the way home, just as he had dragged the python.

So the warrior married the woman, and there were no more bachelors left in Oba. However, Kalameleme was often heard muttering (when he was sure his wife was not within earshot) that he would have preferred to remain single.

Why the Pig Is in the Doghouse

– A Folktale from Arunachal Pradesh

There was, at the dawn of civilization, a man who shared his house with a pig and a dog. While the man laboured ceaselessly, the animals lazed around the house or took long naps. But they were always around at mealtimes and they had huge appetites.

One day the man lost his temper.

"Neither of you does any work," he yelled, "yet, you eat until you're fit to burst! This won't do!"

The pig and the dog were taken aback. They had never before seen their master in such a foul mood.

"W…What do you want us to do, Master?" whined the pig.

"Go and work in my field," said the man. "Only the one who shows a capacity for hard work, will find a place in my house. The other will have to leave!"

The two hurried to the field. There, the pig that had been badly frightened by his master's threat got to work at once. He

ploughed the field from end-to-end and then from side-to-side. And then, once again from end-to-end.

The dog, on the other hand, had got over his fright. Moreover, he had a plan. So he slept the entire day, getting up only occasionally to look for food or to chase squirrels.

He was asleep, when the pig scrambled out of the field in the evening.

"I've finished," said the pig, prodding him awake.

"I'm waiting for a friend," said the dog, opening one eye. "You go on; I'll catch up with you."

The moment the pig's back was turned, the dog jumped into the field and ran all over it. Then, he ran to catch up with the pig.

They reached home at sundown and their master met them at the front door.

"Well, what did you do?" he demanded.

"I ploughed the field, Master," squealed the pig, "and I think I've done a very good job of it too. You'll be proud of me when you see my work tomorrow!"

"You may go in," said the man. The pig skipped in joyfully, throwing a pitying look at the dog. He wondered how the dog would manage when he was booted out.

But the dog didn't seem worried. He moved closer to the man and whispered, "What a bad liar he is! I know you were not fooled, but I'm amazed at his audacity. How could he claim credit for work that I have done! He did not make the slightest attempt to help me. I did all the work!"

The man did not say a word. He stood thinking for a while, and then he moved aside to let the dog enter.

The man went out very early the next day, and both the pig and the dog knew he had gone to inspect the field. So when they saw him returning some hours later, both of them rushed out to meet him.

"Did you find my work satisfactory, Master," asked the pig, coyly.

"Stop trying to fool me, will you!" snapped the man. "Your work, indeed! All I saw in the field were Dog's footprints. It was he who ploughed the field!"

"D…Dog's footprints!" gasped the pig, uncomprehendingly.

"Come, Dog!" said the man, striding into the house. "From now on, only you may come into the house and stay with me!"

"B… But, Master!" squealed the pig. "It was I who did all the work! Honest!"

"And for that you may stay in my backyard!" sneered the man. "Never dare step into my house again!"

The pig pleaded to be allowed into the house, but his master was unrelenting.

And that is how it has been ever since. The dog has the run of the house, but let a pig try to enter and all hell breaks loose!

The Generous Student

– **A Folktale from China**

Lin Piao stayed absent from classes very often. One day the principal of the college made up his mind to expel him. So he sent for the young man.

Lin arrived just as the principal was about to go for lunch.

"Is this the time to come?" asked the principal, sternly.

"Forgive me, Sir," said Lin, "but I got to college very late today. You see, I found a lump of gold in our field."

"A lump of gold!" said the principal, his eyes popping out. "Oh, my, what are you going to do with it?"

"I decided to build a palatial house, buy several acres of land and several head of cattle," said the student. "I also decided to give you a small sum for the trouble you have taken in educating me."

The principal was pleased and invited Lin to eat with him. The young man ate ravenously, but the principal hardly touched his food. He was wondering how much Lin would give him and if it would be enough to buy that small paddy field that he had always wanted.

"I hope you've kept the gold in a safe place," he said, suddenly coming out of his reverie.

"I never got a chance to do that," said Lin. "It disappeared the moment my mother shook me awake."

"What!" screamed the principal. "You mean it was all a dream?!"

The young man nodded.

The principal controlled himself with a great effort of his will.

"I'm happy you remembered me in your dream," he said, finally. "I hope you remember me when you really get some gold. Now please leave."

It was only when the young man had left that the principal remembered why he had sent for him.

The Unrepentant Rogue

– A Folktale from Madhya Pradesh

The old Thakur was on his deathbed.

All through his life, he had been a notorious mischief-monger, quarrelling with all and sundry, making life miserable for those around him. As his life ebbed away, he sent messages to half a dozen of his most powerful enemies, pleading with them to come to his bedside to forgive him, so that he could die in peace.

So all his enemies arrived pleased that their adversary had at last been humbled. The Thakur cast a remorseful eye on each of them and said in a trembling voice, "Gentlemen, it is exceedingly kind of you to have come at the request of this wretch you see lying in front of you. I have wronged you all and I must atone for it."

His visitors were greatly moved. They said, "Please, Thakur saheb, forget whatever has happened. We all make mistakes. We hold no grudge against you."

"You are great and noble souls," quavered the old man, his eyes brimming with tears. "But unless I receive some token punishment from you, I will not be convinced that you've forgiven me."

"What is it that you want us to do?" asked one of the men.

The Thakur took out a long sharp nail and a hammer from under his pillow.

"Do not refuse a dying man," he pleaded. "I want each of you to place the point of the nail against my throat and tap it lightly. Hurry, I can feel the end approaching."

Not wanting to refuse his dying wish, the men lined up to administer the token punishment. The first three men did it quickly and awkwardly, but with so much care that the nail did not even pierce the skin. The fourth man, however, was so overcome with emotion that he hit the nail harder than he had intended to. The nail pierced the skin and drew blood. This was exactly what the wily Thakur had hoped would happen.

"They've killed me... murderers!" he screamed with all the strength that he could summon, and died.

The six men were arrested on charges of conspiracy to murder and sentenced to long terms in prison.

The Tiger's Knock

– Folktale from Karnataka

Timma's wife had gone to her mother's house and Timma had invited three of his friends for a game of cards.

They played in silence for a while enjoying the cosy comfort of the house. Outside, it was cold and windy and a light rain had started to fall.

Finally one of the men, Vinay, broke the silence.

"Have you heard?" he said and stopped.

"Heard what?" asked Timma.

"About the tiger that goes around knocking on people's doors at night."

"A tiger that knocks on doors!" exclaimed Dondu, the strongest of the group. "I don't believe it!"

"Neither do I," said Vinay hastily. "I just heard it being told, that's all."

Suddenly, there was a knock on the door.

The men froze.

"S… somebody's knocking," said Pico, the fourth man.

Timma got up to open the door.

"No!" said Vinay, catching hold of his hand. "Don't open it! It could be the tiger!"

"Don't talk nonsense!" said Dondu.

"Tigers don't knock on doors – or do they?"

"This one does," said Vinay, " they say it calls out the person's name too. When the person opens the door – it tears him apart!"

The knocking began again.

"I… It's calling out… I mean I heard my name being called," said Timma, the blood draining from his face.

"Close the windows," whispered Pico. Vinay rushed to obey him.

The knocking became louder and then stopped.

Now, as the reader might have guessed it was Timma's wife who had returned and was knocking on the door.

When her husband failed to respond, she became worried and called the neighbours.

They decided to break down the door.

The men inside thought the tiger had redoubled its efforts to get in and cowered in fright. Finally, the door gave way under the combined assault of the people outside and Timma's wife and her neighbours streamed in.

Timma and his friends however, did not wait to see who had entered.

The fear-crazed men rushed to the rear of the house, flung open the back door and ran screaming into the night.

God Provides

– A Folktale from Andhra Pradesh

A generous king once ruled, in the land of Andhra. Every day, two beggars used to come to him for alms and he always gave them food and money.

On receiving the alms one of them, the older one, would say, "God provides."

The other beggar, the younger of the two, would say, "Our king provides."

One day, the king gave them more money than usual, whereupon the older man cried out lustily, "God provides."

This annoyed the king who thought, "It is I who am feeding him, and he keeps saying, 'God provides, God provides'. It is time he learnt who his real benefactor is."

The next day, after he had given them alms, he asked the beggars to go by a little-used road, instead of their usual one.

"I have provided for one of you," he said, "God will provide for the other."

He made sure that the one who always praised him went first. He had ordered that a purse of gold be kept on the road in the beggar's path, so that he would find it.

But as the beggar walked down the road, he wondered why the king had sent him that way.

"Perhaps, he wants me to enjoy the privacy of this road," he thought. "It is indeed a beautiful road and so broad. One can walk with eyes closed."

And he closed his eyes.

As a result, he missed seeing the purse. It was spotted and

picked up by the other beggar, who was coming behind him.

The next day, the king asked the beggars if they had found anything on the road that he had sent them by and he looked meaningfully at the younger man. But the beggar shook his head.

"It was a beautiful road," he said. "But I did not find anything on it."

"But I did," said the other man, "I found a purse of gold. God provides."

Now, the king was even more determined to show the older beggar that he was their true benefactor. So while the beggars were going away, he called the younger one back and gave him a pumpkin.

The pumpkin had been hollowed out and filled with silver coins. But the beggar did not know that. On the way, he sold it to a baniya for a few coins.

The next day, the king asked the beggars if anything eventful had happened the previous day, looking meaningfully at the younger beggar.

"Nothing," said the beggar. "Except that I earned a few more coins than usual, by selling the pumpkin you had so generously given me."

The king tried hard not to show his dismay.

"And you?" he said to the other beggar. "Did you too earn more than usual?"

"I certainly did," said the beggar.

"As I was passing by a baniya's shop, he called me and gave me a pumpkin. When I went home and cut it, I found that it was full of silver. As I always say, God provides."

Two Foolish Men

– A Folktale from Bihar

Once there was a raja, who thought he was the cleverest man in the world.

One day, he took his dewan aside and confided to him that he was tired of the idle chatter of ordinary men, and wanted to converse with somebody who was his intellectual equal. The

dewan, knowing that his royal master would not be able to converse intelligently with even a schoolboy, promised to bring someone. A few days later, he came with a dumb shepherd and told the raja that the man was a genius.

"We shall soon see about that," said the ruler. "As he cannot talk, we will converse in gestures," saying which, he held up one finger. The shepherd raised two fingers in reply.

"Good, good," said the raja and held up three fingers. The shepherd gestured violently to show disagreement, and left.

"He is indeed the wisest of men," said the raja, when the shepherd had gone. "When I held up one finger, I was stating that I stood unrivalled in power. He held up two fingers to remind me that God was more powerful. I held up three fingers to ask if there was anyone beside God and myself. He said no and left."

Everyone marvelled at the shepherd's wisdom. The raja bestowed wealth and honours on him and he lived out the rest of his life in comfort. But he never really understood why the raja had been so good to him.

He often recollected his first meeting with the raja. The raja had held up one finger, which of course meant he wanted one of his sheep. Being a loyal subject he had offered two. But then the raja had asked for three! How could anyone part with all his sheep? He had refused and left the palace.

Sukku Finds a Bride

– A Folktale from Madhya Pradesh

S UKKU wanted to marry, but his mother could find no family willing to give their daughter to her son, as he was very poor.

One day, tired of his constant pleas to find him a wife, she wrapped a thorny log in a sari and kept it upright in a corner of her room. When her son returned from work in the evening, she told him that she had found a bride for him.

Sukku was overjoyed. He wanted to know who she was and when they could get married.

"She's right here, in my room," said his mother. "As for getting married, poor people like us cannot afford such ceremonies. Consider yourself already married."

"Can I see her?" asked Sukku.

"Only from the door. Don't go in. She's very shy."

Sukku peeped into his mother's room and drew back, thrilled.

"She's sitting in a corner with her back turned to me," he whispered.

"She'll get over her shyness in course of time," said his mother. Don't be impatient. Don't ever go near her until she calls you."

She kept a constant watch over the room and whenever Sukku tried to enter, pulled him back. But one day, when she was not looking, Sukku tiptoed into the room and touched the log. One of its thorns pricked him and he drew back his hand with a cry.

His mother quickly led him out of the room.

"She pinched me!" said Sukku, angrily. "She has no respect for me! She deserves to be thrashed!"

"Don't frighten her," said his mother. "I told you not to enter until she had called you. Now go and eat."

Sukku ate listlessly.

Watching him, his mother realized that his mind was in turmoil. Now she regretted having played the trick on him and decided to end the masquerade that very night, before things got out of hand. So before going to bed, she unwrapped the log and heaved it out of the window.

Meanwhile, Sukku tossed about on his cot unable to sleep. He felt remorse for having threatened to beat his wife. Finally, he decided to go and see how she was.

When he stole into his mother's room and found that she was the only person there, he was seized with panic.

"She has gone!" he wailed, shaking his mother awake. "My wife has gone!"

"Naturally," said his mother, quickly gathering her wits. "Didn't you say you would thrash her? She must have got scared and run away."

Sukku ran out of the house calling, "Are you there? Are you there?"

Then seeing a young woman coming towards him, he rushed forward shouting, "Please come home with me. I won't hurt you. I won't come near you until you call me!"

The young woman had run away from home. Sukku's plea went straight to her heart. No one had ever talked so kindly to her before.

"I'll come," she said.

Sukku's mother was astonished to see her son bring home a woman, one moreover, who was prepared to live with him. She took it as an act of God and quickly got them married.

The three of them lived happily ever after.

Immune to Flattery

– A Folktale from Myanmar

A raja was told that, a man who had made a career of flattery was coming to the palace.

"Be on your guard, your majesty," warned his advisers. "This fellow wins the favour of the high and mighty through flattery, and then gets them to part with costly gifts or grants of land."

"I'm too hard-headed to fall for such tricks," said the raja. "Let him come."

When the man came, he recited a verse in the ruler's honour and fell at his feet.

"How honoured I am to be in the same room as the mightiest of monarchs," he intoned. "I find myself blinded by the radiance of your beauty, the glory of your presence, your divine charm, your grace, your elegance…"

He went on in this fashion for about twenty minutes. When he paused for breath, one of the advisers seized the opportunity to have a quick word with his royal master.

"Didn't we warn you, Your Majesty," he said, "he is a glib talker."

"Have no fear," replied the raja. "As I told you it's not easy to trick me. The moment he starts to flatter me, I'll have him thrown out. But so far he has spoken nothing but the truth."

The Four Old Women

– A Folktale from Northern India

F our very old women began quarrelling about who was the greatest among them.

Finally, they went to a young bride and requested her to settle the dispute.

The young bride agreed and asked them to present their case one-by-one.

"I am Mother Hunger. I am the greatest," announced the first woman very proudly.

The bride shook her head in disapproval and said, "What is

so great about hunger? One can overcome it by eating any food, including stale dry *chappatis.*"

"I am Mother Thirst. I am the greatest," asserted the second woman.

"No, you are not," said the bride, "thirst can be quenched even with ditch water."

"I am Mother Sleep. I am the greatest," said the third woman.

But the bride retorted, "One can have sound sleep even on a bed of broken stones," and turned her face away.

Now the fourth woman began to present her case, "I am Mother Hope. I am..."

But even before she could finish the sentence the bride bent down to touch her feet and exclaimed, "You are the greatest! For truly has it been said, where there is life there is hope."

The Three Brothers

– A Folktale from Braj, Northern India

The wife of the headman of a village, died soon after giving birth to a son.

The headman was inconsolable, but was persuaded by his family and friends to marry again, so that the child would have someone to look after him.

Fortunately, his second wife turned out to be a large-hearted and sensible woman, who gave the child all the love and care that he would have received from his own mother. Over the next few years, she presented the headman with two more sons, but her affection for the oldest never diminished. She treated all three boys alike and the two younger ones never realized they had a stepbrother.

When the headman passed away, the widow entrusted the responsibilities of the household and the fields to the eldest son and he managed them so well that the family prospered. This made the neighbours envious. One day, one of them told the widow's sons the truth about their eldest brother. They advised them to drive him away from the house, lest he should deprive them of their share of their father's property. The boys were shocked at the revelation, and frightened by the prospect of losing their share of the property, decided to murder him.

When they told their mother about what they planned to do, she said to them, "Don't bloody your hands; I will get rid of him for you."

That night, when everybody was asleep, she suddenly jumped out of bed and started shouting, "Snake! Snake!"

"Where? Where did you see it, mother?" asked the eldest son, getting up from his mat.

"Alas," said the widow, "I saw it disappearing into your stomach."

The young man turned pale. From that day on, he lost all appetite for food and would lie on his mat the entire day. Soon, he became so weak that he could not even sit up on his mat.

The neighbours rejoiced and took advantage of the situation. They built a wall across the widow's courtyard and claimed a

part of the house as their own. In the fields, they shifted their boundaries to enclose large portions of the widow's lands.

The younger sons could not deal with the situation and one day, they said to their mother, "If our elder brother was not bed-ridden, such terrible things would not have happened to us."

The widow kept quiet, but in the dead of the night she again started shouting, "Snake! Snake!"

Everyone woke up.

"Where... where did you see it mother?" asked the eldest son, weakly.

"Son, I saw it coming out of your stomach," replied the woman. "It disappeared into the darkness."

From that day on, the condition of the eldest son started improving. Soon, he was able to walk into the courtyard, where he saw the new wall. "Who has built this!" he thundered.

The neighbours came running and meekly pulled down the wall.

The following week, he went to the family fields and seeing the new boundaries shouted, "Who has done this!"

The neighbours trembled in fear and quickly vacated the land they had grabbed.

The widow and her three sons lived in peace and harmony ever after.

The Fault Finder

– A Folktale from Western Uttar Pradesh

A boorish farmer used to beat his wife every day, on some pretext or the other, making her life miserable. One day, her elder sister paid her a visit. The farmer's wife poured out her woes to her and expressed a wish to leave her husband.

"Don't be hasty," advised her sister. "You have to be careful not to upset him, that's all. I'll show you how to handle him. I'll do everything today."

She cooked, washed the clothes, swept the floor and put the farmer's cot in the open courtyard with a clean sheet spread on it.

When the farmer returned in the evening, he found the house spick and span. His wife served him the hot, tasty food that her sister had kept ready for him and he ate to his heart's content. Then he went to his cot and lay down.

"See, what did I tell you?" said the older woman to her sister. "He's like a lamb. You have to treat him well, that's all. Now he'll go to sleep and..."

Suddenly, they heard him calling.

His wife hurried out and saw him looking intently at the stars overhead.

"What is that white strip up there?" he asked, pointing to the sky.

"Oh, that is the Milky Way," said his wife, and remembering what her grandmother had told her, added, "It is the heavenly path on which Lord Indra's elephant goes to the river every night."

"What?" shouted the farmer. "You've put my cot directly under the Milky Way! What if the elephant stumbles and falls on me, you miserable woman...!"

And to the horror of the woman watching from the house, he sprang up from the cot and started beating his wife.

What a Rat!

– A Folktale from Nagaland

Nagas believe that rice was introduced to man by the rat.

Back in the days when man lived on roots and fruits, a rat accosted a Naga and made a deal with him.

"I'll show you something that is good to eat," said the rat, "but you will have to promise that when I die, you will give me a decent burial."

"I promise, I promise, I promise!" said the Naga. "Show me this food!"

The rat took him to a place where wild rice was growing.

"Learn to cultivate it and you will never go hungry," said the rat. "And remember your promise."

Man began to grow rice, and his life took a turn for the better.

One day, the rat that had made the deal with the man decided to test his honesty.

Seeing the man coming, it lay down in his path and pretended to be dead.

"Farewell, my friend," said the man, when he saw the seemingly lifeless body of the rat, and going up to the animal kicked it unceremoniously, into a nearby river.

"So this is how you keep your promise!" spluttered the rat, swimming out of the river, "I'll never forgive you for this! Any rice that you grow I'll eat as much of it as I can, and whatever I can't eat, I'll contaminate with my droppings!"

And that, they say, is the reason why rice godowns are always infested with rats and why rat droppings constitute such a high percentage of the contaminants in the grain.

The Right to Say No

– **A Folktale from Rajasthan**

One day, a beggar knocked at the door of a house.
When a woman opened the door, he asked her for alms.

"I've nothing to give you," said the woman, "please go!"

The woman, who was newly married, lived with her mother-in-law. When her mother-in-law heard her refusing alms to the beggar, she was furious.

"Who are you to refuse alms to this man!" she demanded. "I'm the mistress of the house!"

Thus chastened, the daughter-in-law fled to her room.

"Thank you, kind lady," said the beggar, ingratiatingly.

"All I asked for was a coin to buy food. I did not know she was not the mistress of the house."

"She's not!" snapped the woman. "She had no right to refuse you alms. I'm in charge here, and let me tell you something, you're not getting a paisa from me!"

And with that, she slammed the door in the beggar's face.

The Master of Pantomime

– A Folktale from Kerala

In the dance form of Kerala, known as Kathakali, the dancer communicates through facial expressions and eloquent movements of the hands and body.

There was once a famous exponent of Kathakali in Kerala. His name was Parameshwaran, but he was known as the Chakiar of Ammannoor.

One day, the Chakiar was walking on the beach, when the British resident's dog came bounding towards him. Afraid that it might attack him, the Chakiar pretended to pick up a stone and mimed the action of throwing the stone with great force. The dog stopped in its track and went back howling to its master. The resident was very angry and admonished the Chakiar for throwing a stone at his dog.

"I threw no stone, sir," said the man, humbly. "I merely pretended to throw one."

"Then why did my dog howl?" snapped the Britisher.

"It thought it had been struck by the imaginary stone," explained the Chakiar.

"I don't believe you!" said the resident. "My dog does not have such a strong imagination!"

A look of theatrical anger came upon the Chakiar's face. Then to the resident's horror, he stooped, seemingly to pick up a stone and flung his arm forward.

The resident felt as if he had been hit on the forehead with a stone. He reeled back and fell to the ground. Then, he touched his forehead gingerly to see if it was bleeding.

"Don't be alarmed, sir," said the Chakiar. "You've not been hit. I did not pick up a stone, nor throw one. I merely performed the actions."

The resident got shakily to his feet. He apologized for his behaviour and congratulated the Chakiar on his mastery of the art of pantomime.

The Hardened Criminal

– A Folktale from Myanmar

Shan was going to his grandfather's house that was a day and a half away from his own.

He walked the entire day and towards nightfall, he lay down on a patch of grass near the road. Thinking it unsafe to keep his money on his person, he took out the few coins that he had in his pocket and kept them under a rock. Then he rolled over and went to sleep.

Unfortunately, a woodcutter passing by saw what he had done and when Shan was asleep, stole the money.

When the boy awoke the next morning and saw that his money was missing, he began to cry. People passing by stopped to find out what had happened. When they learnt that he had been robbed, they took him to the chief of their village.

The chief was a wise old man who commanded great respect in the village. After hearing the boy's story he ordered his men to bring the stone under which the money had been kept, to the court.

"I'll come there to try the case," he said.

The villagers were intrigued. They wondered why the chief had ordered the stone to be brought to the court. So by the time he reached the court, it was packed with people.

The chief took his seat and asked the village policeman, who was standing there to produce the suspect.

"I... I have no suspect, Sir," said the policeman, uneasily. "I haven't had time to investigate."

"Didn't you bring the stone?" said the chief.

"Ah, yes, the stone!" said the policeman, relieved.

He hastily brought the stone and placed it in front of the chief.

"Now, then," said the chief, addressing the stone. "Do you deny taking the boy's money?"

The people looked at each other, perplexed. Some of them felt that their chief had gone mad. Why else would he talk to a stone?

"The suspect does not answer," said the chief to the court

clerk. "That is an admission of guilt. I have a feeling we are dealing with a hardened criminal."

A man in the court, amused by the chief's remark, began to giggle, but quickly stopped when the chief looked in his direction.

"I find the stone guilty," said the chief. "As punishment it will be given twenty lashes with the whip and then its head will be cut off!"

The man, who had giggled could not control himself and burst out laughing. Others around him began to laugh too and soon the entire court was rocking with laughter.

"Silence!" roared the chief, banging his fist on the table. "How dare you laugh at my decision? This is contempt of court for which you cannot go unpunished. I hereby sentence you all to pay a fine of one penny each. Please come one by one and place your money on my table."

Soon there was a small pile of pennies on the table. The chief called the boy and pushed the pile towards him.

"Take it," he said. "It is to recompense you for the trouble you have been put to."

Shan was overjoyed. He was being given more money than he had lost.

Before the villagers sent him off, he was given a sumptuous meal. Then they took him to the village square to see the flogging. But after only a few strokes of the whip, Shan felt so sorry for the stone that he begged the chief to show it mercy.

The chief relented and the stone was let off with a warning.

Inviting Trouble

– A Folktale from Thailand

There was a fig tree in the grounds of an old monastery and it produced fruits that were big and sweet.

The chief of the monastery was fond of figs, so fond of them in fact that though he could not possibly eat all the figs the tree produced, he would not allow anyone to take a single fruit from it. He did not mind if the figs fell and rotted on the ground.

One day, the monk had a visitor, a man from the village.

"I've come to request you to give me some figs," said the man.

"That's out of the question," said the monk.

"Never mind," said the man. "Forget that I asked. But do not refuse my second request. Please join me for dinner, the day after tomorrow. My brother-in-law has brought some dried shark fins from Thailand and I plan to make shark fin soup."

"Shark fin soup!" exclaimed the monk. He loved good food and shark fin soup was a delicacy only the rich could afford.

"I'll certainly come and... er... about the figs... you may take a few."

The man filled a large basket with the figs and left.

The next day, another man from the village called on the monk. He too asked for figs and was refused.

"Never mind," said the man. "It's not important. My main reason for coming was to invite you to my house for dinner, the day after tomorrow. My cousin has brought sausages from China and I would like to share the delicacy with you."

"I haven't eaten sausages in years," said the monk, drooling, "I'll certainly come, and as for the figs... you may take a few."

The next day, the first man came to take the monk to his house. But hardly had they stepped out of the monastery, than the second man appeared.

"The sausages smelt so good," he said, "I couldn't wait another day. My wife's cooking them. I've come to take you."

"He's coming to my house," said the first man, taking hold of the monk's hand. "Come on, Sir."

"You promised to come to my house!" said the second man taking hold of the monk's other hand. "You can't let me down. I've told everyone you're coming."

"Let go of him!" shouted the first man. "He's coming to my house!"

Then both men started shouting at each other and pulling the monk in opposite directions.

"Let me go!" squealed the monk, pulling himself free. He was panting and gasping. Never had he been handled so roughly. Never had anyone fought for his company either. So he was not entirely displeased.

"Let's not fight," he said, "I'll come to both houses, in turn."

Each man insisted that he come to his house first. They caught hold of him again and began pulling him this way and that. This was too much for the monk.

"Enough!" he screamed. "Enough! Let go of me both of you! I'm not coming to either house!"

"Not coming to either house?" said the men, looking disappointed.

"No!" said the monk. "I've lost my appetite. Please go... please."

The men went away. When they were out of sight of the monastery, they burst into laughter and began to clap each other on the back. They were old friends, who liked to play tricks on people. Being poor, all they had been cooking at home was rice. And of course for dessert there were the figs.

Transformation

– A Folktale from Kashmir

Abdullah hated hard work, so he could never hold down a job for more than a month or two. There were long periods when he was out of work. Seeing him sprawled on the bed when he should have been out working, infuriated his wife. There were frequent and violent quarrels in the house.

A friend, who happened to be present when one of these fights broke out, offered Abdullah words of advice, when he next met him.

"You're too soft," he said. "I would never allow my wife to talk to me in the manner that yours does. The next time, she raises her voice glare at her, and say, "'I've had enough! I can't stay in this house anymore,' and stride towards the door."

"And then?"

"And then see the change in her! She'll be transformed! She'll fall at your feet, and beg forgiveness. Never again will she try to pick a quarrel with you!"

As it happened, a blazing row erupted between husband and wife, the very next day. Abdullah, remembering his friend's advice, glared at his wife, and said, "I've had enough! I can't stay in this house anymore!"

His wife continued shouting and throwing things. Abdullah thought that perhaps she had not heard.

"I'm leaving," he thundered. "Never to return!"

The announcement made no impression on the woman, whose rage continued unabated. Abdullah's heart sank. Now what was he to do? He wished his friend were around to advise him. He moved slowly towards the door, hoping his wife would realize that he meant what he said, and come rushing to stop him.

But no such thing happened.

"I'm leaving!" he shouted, opening the door.

Then, of course, he had to keep going. Slowly, he moved towards the road, expecting his wife to come running out to stop

him, at every step. But the door of his house remained firmly shut, and Abdullah, realized with a sinking feeling that his wife had no intention of stopping him.

He returned home several hours after sunset. His wife had gone to bed, but his dinner was laid out on the table. Having had nothing to eat the entire day, he ate ravenously, and gratefully.

Early next morning, he set out to look for work. The humiliating experience he had gone through had changed his outlook on life.

He had been transformed.

Top Answers

– Adapted from a Folktale from Nepal

Bhupendra Prasad had spent a huge sum on his only son's wedding that had been celebrated with pomp and splendour.

A few weeks after the wedding, Bhupendra, wanting to test his daughter-in-law's intelligence asked her, "Can you guess how much I spent on your wedding?"

"About the cost of a sack of rice," said the woman.

Her father-in-law's mouth dropped open in astonishment.

"The cost of a sack of rice!" he spluttered. "You foolish girl, I spent a fortune on your wedding!" The woman said nothing.

"She's a nitwit," thought Bhupendra. "A nitwit! My poor son!"

A few weeks later, while they were all going to a relative's wedding, they met up with a funeral procession.

"Who has died?" asked Bhupendra, stopping a mourner.

"Is it just one corpse or a hundred?" asked his daughter-in-law.

Bhupendra, greatly embarrassed by his daughter-in-law's question, walked away without waiting for the mourner's answer.

Presently, they came upon labourers working in a field.

"Looks as if you had a good harvest!" shouted Bhupendra.

"But are you reaping this year's harvest or last year's?" asked his daughter-in-law.

"Your wife is mad!" said Bhupendra to his son. "Mad! She talks nonsense!"

"Does she?"

"Don't pretend you don't know!" roared his father. "Didn't you hear the silly questions she asked?"

"Her questions may not be as silly as they seem," said his son. "Why not ask her to explain?"

Bhupendra did not say anything. But later, when he found

himself alone with his daughter-in-law, he decided to act on his son's advice.

"Tell me," he said, "what did you mean when you asked the mourner whether they were carrying one corpse or a hundred?"

"Some men have scores of dependents," explained the young woman. "When such a man dies many lives are shattered. His dependents die with him, in a way. That is why I asked the mourner if they were carrying one corpse or a hundred."

"What did you mean when you asked those labourers whether they were harvesting this year's crop or last year's?"

"These labourers are perennially in debt," explained the daughter-in-law. "I was enquiring whether they were working to pay off last year's debt or had paid it all and were beginning anew."

Bhupendra now realized that his daughter-in-law, far from being a nitwit, was probably cleverer than he was.

"One last question," he said. "Why did you say I spent only the equivalent of the price of a sack of rice for your wedding, when you know very well I spent a fortune?"

"What you spent on the essentials of the marriage amounted to only a few hundred rupees," smiled the young woman. "The rest you spent to uphold and enhance your prestige. In other words, not on the marriage but on yourself."

Half-Educated

– A Northern Indian Folktale

A jackal met a wolf and the two started talking. "How far have you studied?" asked the wolf, suddenly.

"To tell you the truth, I'm only half-educated," said the jackal.

"Then I'm twice as educated as you," said the wolf. "From now on you, should address me as 'sir'."

Just then, a ferocious tiger stepped out from behind a bush.

"What shall we do... sir?" asked the jackal.

But the wolf was so frightened that he couldn't talk.

"Going somewhere?" growled the tiger, positioning himself to leap.

"We were in fact coming to consult you, sir," said the jackal, thinking quickly. "A dispute has arisen between us and only you, with your superior intelligence could settle it for us."

The tiger was pleased.

"What's this dispute about?" he asked, relaxing.

"I have caught two plump chickens," said the jackal. "My friend says that, as he is more educated than me, he should get one. Now is that fair?"

"How far have you studied?" asked the tiger, looking the wolf up and down.

The wolf's teeth chattered in fright.

"He says he has as many qualifications as there are teeth in his mouth," interpreted the jackal.

"Is that so!" said the tiger. "Then I'm far better educated... see!" And he opened his mouth to show his fearsome teeth.

The sight so unnerved the wolf that his legs gave way and he fell flat on his face.

"He admits you're more educated and is prostrating at your teeth," explained the jackal. "I should prostrate too for the wisdom you've shown in settling our dispute."

"I have?" said the tiger, perplexed.

"Now that you've claimed the chickens for yourself, my friend and I no longer have a dispute," said the jackal. "Please follow me to my house and I'll give you the chickens."

The tiger was delighted. He rarely got to eat chicken. Also, his superior intelligence told him that once he had eaten the chickens, there was nothing to prevent him from eating the jackal and the wolf too.

"Lead the way," he said.

The jackal led him to the mouth of a tunnel in the side of a hill.

"Here we are," he said, "my friend will go in and bring the chickens."

The opening was much too small for the wolf, but he was so eager to gain the safety of the tunnel that, he somehow squeezed himself through it.

When he did not come out for some time, the jackal said he would see what was keeping him and deftly slipped into the tunnel, too.

It took some time for the tiger to realize that he had been tricked. Then he was so furious that, he forgot he was educated and putting his face close to the opening roundly cursed the jackal and flung the choicest abuse at him.

After he had gone, the wolf, helped by the jackal, squeezed out of the tunnel.

He had got his voice back.

"You may be uneducated," he said admiringly, "but you've certainly got brains."

"Thank you," said the jackal. "sir!"

The Challenge

– A Folktale from Assam

A merchant was taking his morning stroll by the seaside, when he saw a man squatting on the beach and filling a cup with sand.

As the merchant watched, the man emptied the contents on a large pile of sand beside him and began filling the cup again. The merchant went up to him and asked him what he was doing.

"I am *Bidhata* (Fate)," said the man. "I am measuring out the food each man is to receive today."

"Can you really do that?" asked the merchant. "I challenge you to withhold my midday meal today!"

"As you wish," replied Bidhata.

The merchant bought a fish, took it home and gave it to his wife. Then he went on to his place of work.

In the afternoon, he came home and sat down to eat.

His wife placed the cooked fish before him.

"Fate said he would withhold my midday meal," thought

the man. "But now, who can stop me from eating this delicious fish?" And he burst out laughing.

His wife thought he was laughing at the way the fish had been prepared and she began to scold him. The merchant got angry. He got up and stormed out of the house.

It was only when he cooled down that he realized the significance of what had happened. Fate had succeeded in withholding his share of food for that afternoon.

The Man Who Wanted Nothing

– **A Folktale from Northwest India**

Wali Dad was a carpenter who lived alone and worked hard the entire day.

His tastes were simple and his wants few, so he spent very little of the money he earned. One day he found that the jar in which he stored his money was full to the brim.

"I must empty it," he thought, "or I'll have no container for my money."

He took the jar to the local jeweller, emptied its contents on the floor and asked the jeweller to give him a bracelet worth the sum. The jeweller gave him a pretty little bracelet made of gold.

Wali Dad wondered what he should do with the bracelet. He saw a merchant, at the head of a line of camels laden with goods, and asked him where he was going.

"To the palace," said the merchant, importantly. "The princess has ordered some clothes."

"Will you give her this bracelet too," said the carpenter,

handing over the bracelet he had bought to him. "Tell her it's a gift from Wali Dad."

The princess liked the bracelet and sent him a camel-load of the finest silks in return.

"What will I do with these silks?" groaned Wali Dad, when the merchant brought the heavily-laden camel to him.

"Give them to someone else," suggested the merchant.

"Who?"

"Perhaps the Sultan of Kesh."

So Wali Dad sent the silk to the Sultan, who delighted with the gift, sent him six of his finest horses.

Wali Dad sent them on to the princess.

"Who is this Wali Dad? And why is he sending me gifts?" she asked her advisor.

"Probably, somebody who wants to impress you with his wealth," said the advisor. "Send him a gift that he cannot match. That will humble his pride."

The princess sent him 20 mules laden with silver. Not wishing to be burdened by so much wealth, Wali Dad sent the silver to the Sultan. The Sultan was perplexed.

"Who is this Wali Dad? And why is he sending me gifts?" he asked his advisor.

"Probably, somebody who wants to impress you with his wealth," said the advisor. "Send him a gift that he cannot match. That should humble him."

The Sultan sent Wali Dad 20 cartloads of precious stones, which Wali Dad promptly re-routed to the princess. The princess, her curiosity piqued, decided to pay him a visit. She set out secretly, taking only her maid with her. Their enquiries led them to the humble dwelling of the carpenter.

As they were looking around in bewilderment, a handsome man of regal bearing rode towards them. It was the Sultan of Kesh. He too had decided to make the acquaintance of the mysterious Wali Dad. The Sultan and the princess fell in love with each other, at first sight. After a short courtship, they announced their marriage.

Wali Dad was now a famous man. As he refused to go to either of their palaces, the princess and the Sultan sent him a chest full of gold. But it was never delivered. When Wali Dad saw the Sultan's men bringing the gold, he fled the village and was never seen again.

The Promise

– **A Folktale from Norway**

A youth bought a keg of beer for his grandfather and was rolling it home.

On the way, he met a tall, dark man with bloodshot eyes.

"What have you got there?" he asked the boy.

"Beer. Once a month, I take a keg of beer for my grandfather. It's his only weakness."

"Let me have some," said the man.

"Er... whom do I have the honour of addressing?"

"I am Death!"

"Help yourself, Your Eminence," said the boy. "I'm one of your greatest admirers. You deal fairly with all – rich or poor, without favouring any one."

Death drank the whole keg, but the boy said nothing.

"I must recompense you," said Death, wiping his mouth with the back of his hand. "I'll give you the power of healing. Whenever you are called to the bedside of a dying person, look for me. If I'm seated at the person's feet, it means I will permit his recovery. In that case, all you have to do is give the person a glass of water and his health will be restored. However, if I'm seated at the person's head, immediately take your leave. There is no hope for such a person."

"What about me?" asked the youth, "I hope you will allow me many years on Earth."

"I will come for you only when you call me," promised Death.

The youth became famous as a healer in the months that followed. Whenever anyone was dying the youth was sent for. If he saw Death sitting at the person's feet, he would give the person a glass of water and the person would recover. But if he saw Death sitting at the head of the bed, he would say that nothing could be done and withdraw.

One day, he received a call from the palace. The princess had contracted a mysterious fever that was sapping her strength. The royal doctors had given up all hope of her recovery. When the youth entered the room, he saw Death sitting there, at the head of the bed. He hastily backed out of the room. But the girl's father, the king would not let him go.

"Heal her and I'll make you my son-in-law and heir," he promised.

The youth was sorely tempted. He went into the room again. Death was dozing and did not see him. The boy lifted the princess from the bed went round to the other side and kept her down again, so that now Death was sitting at her feet. Picking up a glass of water, he put it to her lips. She began drinking and as she did, the colour began to return to her cheeks.

"You have tricked me," said Death, waking up from his slumber. "Now I'll have to take you instead!"

And with that he disappeared.

The youth was not unduly worried. Death had given him his word that he would not come for him, until he was called and the boy had no intention of calling him, ever! He was dined and feted and made much of at the palace and when night fell, was shown to a large bedroom, where he fell asleep the moment his head touched the pillow.

When he awoke the next morning, he saw some writing on the wall.

He went closer to look and read aloud, "Take me, Death."

He instantly knew he had been tricked. But it was too late. He turned around and there was Death, with his bloodshot eyes.

"You called and I have come," he said, grinning. "Let's go."

In Pursuit of Beni Madho

– A Footnote from History

Rana Beni Madho of Baiswara was one of those who took up arms against the British, in 1857. The chieftain proved a formidable foe and continued to harass the British, long after the national uprising had been suppressed.

In the second half of 1858, an advance party of a British force, led by Lord Clyde and Sir Hope Grant, entered Beni Madho's fort in triumph, but found only a beggar and an elephant there. The Rana had fled the previous night. Thereafter, the British engaged him in two battles. In the second one, at Bheera Govindpur, on December 19, 1858, the Rana was wounded, but escaped.

One night, as the weary British soldiers were huddled around their campfires, resting after another exhausting day spent in pursuit of the Rana, a soldier suddenly sang:

Where have you been all day?

Beni Madho, O Beni Madho!

Another voice piped up,

Why are you so scared of British pluck?

Beni Madho, O Beni Madho!

Because to beat you is not my luck

Beni Madho, O Beni Madho!

–finished a third.

Finally, news came that the Rana was camping on the banks of the River Rapti.

The British hurried there, but the Rana crossed the Rapti and escaped into Nepal.

That night the soldiers sang:

Why are you so scared of British pluck?

Beni Madho, O Beni Madho!

Because to beat you is not my luck

Beni Madho, O Beni Madho!

And that's very sad, oh, very sad

Beni Madho, O Beni Madho!

Nobody knows what happened to Beni Madho after he crossed into Nepal, but the song about him became famous!

Why Crows Are Black

– A Folktale from Burma

The Sun, while going on his daily rounds, saw a princess and fell in love with her.

Whenever he could slip away from the heavens, he would take human form and go down to the princess to spend some time with her. The princess too became quite fond of him and would wait for him to come.

One day, the Sun decided to send her a blood-red ruby, as a token of his love for her. He put the gem in a silken bag, and calling a crow that was flying past, asked the bird to deliver the gem to his beloved. Crows had milky white feathers in those days and it was considered auspicious, if a crow came anywhere near you. So the Sun was pleased that he had found a crow to deliver the gem.

As the crow sped through the sky with the silken bag, the aroma of food reached its nostrils. Looking down, it saw that a wedding feast was in progress, and immediately it was distracted from its mission. Food was one thing it could never resist!

Alighting on a tree nearby, it hung the bag on a twig and went off to find some food.

While the crow was feasting, a merchant passing by saw the bag on the tree, and knocked it down with a pole.

When he opened the bag and saw its contents, he almost swooned in joy. Quickly pocketing the ruby, he filled the bag with dried cow dung that was lying there, and then deftly returned the bag to the branch.

It was all done so quickly that the crow missed all the action. After having its fill, it flew up to the tree, and picking up the bag, took it to the princess. She was in the garden. When the crow gave her the bag, she took it eagerly, knowing that it was from the Sun. But when she saw its contents, she reeled back in shock and anger.

Believing that it was the Sun's way of telling her that he did not care for her, she flung the bag away, rushed to her palace, and never came out again.

When the Sun learnt of what had happened, he was furious. So great was his anger that when he turned his scorching gaze on the crow, its feathers were burned black.

Its feathers have been black ever since.

However, the ruby did not stay with the man who stole it. It fell out of his pocket and rolled into a deep pit.

Men have been trying to dig it out ever since. Many precious stones have been found in the process, making Burma (now Myanmar) one of the richest sources of rubies and sapphires.

But the ruby that the Sun sent to the princess has yet to be found.

Struck by Lightning

– A Folktale from China

Once upon a time, a valet was riding behind his master, the aristocratic Chen Yu.

Chen Yu turned round and when he saw his valet lagging far behind, he yelled at him to ride faster. With great effort, the valet caught up with his master.

"Stay right behind me!" roared Chen Yu.

"My horse is old, master," said the valet, "it cannot keep up with yours."

"That's because you've not fed it!" said Chen Yu, angrily, and gave the lad such a blow on his head that, it nearly unhorsed him.

They continued on their journey. Chen Yu's anger soon subsided, but the valet smouldered. It was not the first time his master had hit him. He had begun to resent being used as a punching bag.

As he brooded, the sky became overcast and it began to thunder. Chen Yu was afraid of thunder and looked up fearfully at the sky.

When it thundered again, he closed his eyes tight and hid his face in the horse's mane. His valet noticed his discomfort and a mischievous idea entered his head.

When next it thundered, the valet rode up behind his master and gave him a blow on the back of his head, at the same time shouting, "Lightning!"

Chen Yu thought he had been hit by lightning and slumped onto the back of his horse.

After some time, he raised his head again. When again it thundered, the valet gave him another blow, shouting as before. This happened again and again. On the tenth occasion, the aristocrat fell from his horse and became unconscious.

The valet dismounted and sat beside him. He felt remorse for what he had done. After all, the man was his master and also much older than him. When Chen Yu began to stir, the boy quickly lay down and closed his eyes. Chen Yu woke up and was pleased to see that his valet too had been knocked unconscious. He began to shake him. The lad opened his eyes and pretended to be dazed.

"What happened, master?" he said.

"Lightning hit you just once and you became unconscious!" laughed Chen Yu, "I was hit ten times before I fell."

When the storm had subsided, they resumed their journey. Chen Yu felt that the gods had punished him for his cruelty to his manservant and from then on he never hit the valet again.

The Hundred Pounds

– A Folktale from Ireland

John Curran was a famous Irish lawyer of the last century.
Many stories are told of his wit and wisdom. This is one of them.

A farmer once approached Curran for help to get his money back from an innkeeper.

"This is my first visit to the city," explained the farmer. "I gave a hundred pounds to the innkeeper for safekeeping, but now he says that he does not remember me giving him any money."

"Give him another hundred pounds for safekeeping," advised the lawyer, "but this time, do it in the presence of a witness, preferably a priest."

The farmer got hold of a priest and in his presence deposited a hundred pounds with the innkeeper. Then he returned to Curran.

"I've done as you advised," he said.

"Good," said Curran. "Now go and demand your money, but go alone."

The farmer went back to the inn and asked for his money. The innkeeper, remembering that there had been a witness to the deposit, reluctantly handed over the hundred pounds.

The farmer rushed back to Curran's office.

"I've got it," he said. "But my first hundred pounds are still with him."

"You'll get that too," said Curran. "Ask him for it. But this time take your witness with you."

When the farmer asked for the money in the presence of the priest, the innkeeper was flabbergasted. He could not deny having received a hundred pounds from the farmer and if he said that he had returned it, people would start doubting his integrity.

Very reluctantly, he returned the money he owed the farmer.

Tales That Inspire

Treble Trouble

A man was caught stealing a bag of onions and taken before a judge.

The judge gave him a choice of three punishments; eat the onions he had stolen at one sitting; submit to a hundred lashes of the whip; or pay a fine.

The man said he would eat the onions. He began confidently enough but after eating a few, his eyes began to burn, his nose started running and his mouth felt as if it were on fire.

"I can't eat the onions," he said. "Give me the lashes instead."

But after he had received a few strokes, he began to turn and twist to avoid the whip.

"I can't bear it!" he screamed, finally. "I'll pay the fine."

So he paid the fine and was let off. But he became the laughing-stock of the city for having taken three punishments for the same crime.

Fear

– Aesop's Fable

There was a lion, which feared nothing except the crowing of cocks.

A chill would go down his spine, whenever he heard a cock crowing.

One day he confessed his fear to the elephant who was greatly amused.

"How can the crowing of a cock hurt you?" he asked the lion. "Think about it!"

Just then, a mosquito began circling the elephant's head, frightening him out of his wits.

"If it gets into my ear I'm doomed!" he shrieked, flailing at the insect with his trunk.

Now, it was the lion's turn to feel amused.

Rope Trick

A Jat and his family were on their way to the city. At noon, on the second day of their journey, they came upon a huge banyan tree and decided to rest under it for a while.

The Jat did not want to stay idle, so he decided to make a rope. He sent his eldest son to a town nearby to buy jute; he sent his second son to buy vegetables, and the third son to buy provisions. He assigned duties to his daughters-in-law too. One was sent to fetch water; another, firewood. The third one was asked to knead the dough.

When he had got all the materials that he needed, the Jat sat under the tree to make the rope. Now, there was a giant living on the tree. He had been observing the Jat and his family ever since they had camped under his tree. He wondered why the man was making a rope. Finally, unable to contain his curiosity, he got down and asked him.

The Jat concealed his fear and kept on working. Looking defiantly at the giant, he said he was making the rope to tie him.

The giant was shaken. Though big, he was timid at heart. He fell at the Jat's feet and begged for mercy.

"I'll make you rich," he said, and digging up a chest of treasure, gave it to him.

The Jat was overjoyed. He cut short his journey and returned to his village, a rich man.

When his neighbour heard how he had come by his wealth, he immediately gathered his own family and set out for the giant's abode.

There, he began issuing instructions to his sons and daughters-in-law. But his sons refused to leave the shade of the tree to run errands and his daughters-in-law just ignored him.

He had to do everything himself.

Eventually, he got all the materials he needed and he sat down under the tree to make the rope.

He was thrilled when the giant descended from the tree.

"Why are you making that rope?" asked the giant.

"Why else but to tie you," said the man.

The giant smiled.

"So you're afraid," said the man. "Better give me a chest of treasure or I won't spare you."

"If your own family is not afraid of you why should I be?" laughed the giant, climbing back onto his tree.

"Tie your sons and daughters-in-law, before thinking of tying anybody else."

Costly Gifts

One day, a king stepped out of the gates of his palace and found a man standing there.

The man had a plump chicken in his hands. On seeing the king, he bowed respectfully and said, 'Maharaj, I gambled in your name and won this chicken. It belongs to you. Please accept it."

"Give it to my poultry keeper," said the king.

A few days later, the king saw the man standing outside the gates again. This time he had a goat with him. "I won this goat in your name, Maharaj," he said after saluting the ruler. "It belongs to you."

The king was pleased.

"Give it to my goat keeper," he said.

Some weeks later, the man was at the palace gates once again.

This time he had two men with him.

"I lost 500 varahas to each of these men, while playing in your name, Maharaj," said the man. "I have no money to pay them."

The king realized he had made a mistake in accepting the man's gifts on the previous occasions. Now, he could not refuse to help him. He paid off the two men and warned the gambler never to play in his name again.

The Old Woman and
Her Rooster

An old woman noticed that her rooster crowed just before sun-up, each day and she came to the conclusion that, the sun rose because her cock crowed!

The woman had until then led a quiet and uneventful life. Now, she began to put on airs and people began to notice a marked arrogance in her manner. One day, she decided it was time that she showed the villagers how dependent they were on her. Accordingly, she stole out of the village with the cock and took up residence in a forest nearby. The next day, when the cock crowed and a little later the sun rose, she concluded that the sun had followed her to the forest.

"Now, they will realize who was making the sun rise," she thought gleefully and waited for the villagers to come and beg her to return.

But of course, nobody came. Some days later, she sneaked down to the village to see what was happening. When she saw that the sun was shining as brightly as ever there and realized that nobody had even noticed her absence, she was cured of her pride forever!

Greedy Trader

There was a merchant, who was engaged in trade with a number of coastal towns, because of which he had to travel extensively by boat.

One day, a friend asked him if he could swim.

"That I cannot," said the merchant.

"You should learn," said his friend. "I know a man, who could teach you swimming in three days."

"I don't have three days to spare," said the merchant. "Time is money."

"Then always carry two empty drums with you," advised the friend. "They'll keep you afloat if your boat should capsize."

The merchant followed his friend's advice. Whenever he travelled by boat, he always took two empty drums with him.

Then one day, it happened just as his friend had foreseen; his boat was caught in a squall, far out at sea.

The merchant, realizing that he could be washed overboard by the waves, lashed himself to the two drums and prepared for the worst. Then he thought, why not save some of the cargo? He was carrying rice. He quickly threw some sacks of the grain into each of the drums. It didn't make them too heavy. So he was tempted to throw in some more, and then some more, till they were filled to capacity.

At that moment, a huge wave knocked him overboard, along with the drums. And he sank like a stone.

The Fisherman Who Rose Too High

A fisherman, enfeebled with age, could no longer go out to sea, so he began fishing in the river. Every morning, he would go down to the river and sit there fishing the entire day. In the evening, he would sell whatever he had caught, buy food for himself and then go home. It was a hard life for an old man.

One hot afternoon, while he was trying to keep awake, a large bird, with silvery feathers, alighted on a rock, near him.

It was Kaha, the heavenly bird.

"Have you no one to care for you, grandpa?" asked the bird.

"Not a soul."

"You should not be doing such hard work at your age," said the bird. "From now on, I'll bring you a big fish every evening. Sell it and live in comfort."

True to her word, the bird began to drop a large fish at his doorstep, every evening. The fisherman only had to take it to the market and sell it. As big fish were in great demand, he was soon rolling in money.

He bought a cottage near the sea and engaged a servant to cook for him. His wife had died, some years earlier. Now, he decided to marry again and began to look for a suitable woman.

One day, he heard the royal crier make an announcement.

"Our king has news of a great bird called Kaha," announced the crier. "Whoever can give information about this bird and help catch it, will be rewarded with half the gold in the royal treasury and half the kingdom!"

The fisherman was very tempted by the reward. Half the kingdom would make him a prince!

"Why does the king want the bird?" he asked.

"He has lost his sight," explained the crier. "A wise man has advised him to bathe his eyes in the blood of a Kaha bird. Do you know where it can be found?"

"No... I mean... no, no..."

Torn between greed and his sense of gratitude to the bird, the fisherman could not give a coherent reply. The crier, sensing that he knew something about the bird, informed the king. The king had him brought to the palace.

"If you have information about the bird, tell me," urged the king. "I will reward you handsomely and if you help catch it, I will personally crown you king of half my domain."

"I will get the bird for you," cried the fisherman, suddenly making up his mind, "But Kaha is strong. I'll need help."

The king sent a dozen men with him.

That evening, when the bird came with the fish, the fisherman called out to her to wait.

"You drop the fish and go, but I never get a chance to thank you for all that you've done for me," he said. "Today, I've laid out a feast for you inside. Please alight and come in."

The Kaha was reluctant to accept the invitation, but the fisherman pleaded so earnestly that she finally gave in, and alighted.

The moment she was on the ground, the fisherman grabbed one of her legs and shouted to the soldiers hiding in his house to come out. They rushed to his aid, but their combined effort could not keep the Kaha down. She rose into the air, with the fisherman still clinging onto her leg.

By the time he realised it, he was being carried away. The fisherman was too high in the air to let go. He hung on grimly, and neither he nor the Kaha were ever seen again.

Filling a Sieve with Water

Ateacher had given a discourse on creative thinking. Later, his disciples approached him and asked him to set them a problem that required them to think creatively. The sage gave them a sieve and asked them to fill it with water at the sea, nearby. They were gone for a long time. Finally, he went down to the beach to see what they were doing, and found them seated morosely around the sieve.

They scrambled to their feet, when they saw him.

"You've set us an impossible task, sir," said the oldest of the disciples. "It's just not possible to fill a sieve with water."

"Are you sure?" asked the teacher, picking up the sieve. "Sometimes, it helps to step back and view the problem from a different angle."

He waded into the water and threw the sieve far out into the sea. It sank.

"There!" said the teacher. "It's full of water now."

The Wise Old Man

A wealthy man requested an old scholar to wean his son away from his bad habits.

The scholar took the youth for a stroll through a garden. Stopping suddenly, he asked the boy to pull out a tiny plant growing there. The youth held the plant between his thumb and forefinger and pulled it out. The old man then asked him to pull out a slightly bigger plant. The youth pulled hard and the plant came out, roots and all.

"Now pull out that one," said the old man pointing to a bush.

The boy had to use all his strength to pull it out.

"Now take this one out," said the old man, indicating a guava tree.

The youth grasped the trunk and tried to pull it out. But it would not budge.

"It's impossible," said the boy, panting with the effort.

"So it is with bad habits," said the sage, "when they are young it is easy to pull them out, but when they take hold they cannot be uprooted."

The session with the old man changed the boy's life.

Learning from the Enemy

Asamurai warrior slew his master in a fit of rage. He repented immediately, but the deed was done and he knew that if he was caught he would be put to death. He fled.

His wanderings took him to a remote village that was separated from the rest of the world, by a mountain. The path across the mountain was narrow and treacherous. Many villagers had lost their lives, while traversing it. The murderer decided to

atone for his sin, by single-handedly cutting a road through the mountain to end the isolation of the village.

He worked from dawn to dusk and in four years had penetrated halfway into the mountain. One morning, when he was hard at work in the tunnel, a young man called out to him to come out. He was the son of the man, who had been murdered. He wanted revenge.

"I deserve to die," said the former samurai. "Slay me by all means, but wait until I've completed this tunnel."

The young man agreed to wait. He watched fascinated as day-after-day the samurai laboured, at a seemingly impossible task. The rocks he was digging through were so massive that at the end of a day's work, they seemed not to have been touched at all. The young man began to develop a grudging respect for his enemy's tenacity and determination. Eventually, he found himself helping the man – digging side-by-side with him and carrying out the rubble.

Years passed and then one day, the two men broke through to the other side. The mountain had been conquered at last and the centuries-old isolation of the village had been ended.

"Now I am ready to die," said the samurai, kneeling before the young man. "Cleave my head in two."

The youth raised his sword with a cry, the blood rushing to his head. At last his father's death would be avenged. But he found that he could not bring himself to do it. Slowly, he lowered his sword.

"You're a murderer," he said. "But I've learnt much from you in these last few years. How can I harm my teacher?"

And he sheathed his sword and walked away.

The Angry Young Man

There was a boy, who was very quick-tempered. One day, his father gave him a bag of nails and a hammer.

"Hammer a nail into the fence every time you lose your temper," he said.

So every time he blew his top, the boy would go out into the garden and hammer a nail into the wooden fence. This made him acutely conscious of his bad temper, and he began to make attempts to control it. He found himself putting fewer and fewer nails into the fence, with each passing day.

Finally, one evening, he realized that he did not have to go to the fence even once.

The next morning, he gave the nails and the hammer back to his father, telling him he did not need them anymore, as he had learnt to control his temper.

"Very good," said his father. "Now pull out all the nails from the fence."

The boy spent the greater part of the morning pulling out the nails, but finally, he had accomplished his task. He gave the nails to his father.

"So many!" said the man. "Come let us see what they have done to the fence."

Together, they examined the holes left by the nails in the fence.

"Anger may die down," said the man to his son, "but the harm it has done does not vanish so easily. It remains like these holes."

It was a lesson the boy never forgot. His volatile temper was not easily tamed, but eventually he developed a calm and peaceable disposition.

Prince Charming

There was once a prince, who was besotted with his own beauty. If any traveller came to the palace, he would ask him, "Have you ever seen anyone as handsome as me?"

No one ever had. One day, an obsequious traveller said to him, "I don't think even a god could be as handsome as you."

This made the prince very happy and he went around telling everyone that he was more handsome than any god.

One day, he had two visitors, who identified themselves as gods.

"We have come to see if you are as handsome as you claim," they explained.

"Am I not?" he asked.

"We visited you earlier in the day when you were asleep," said one of the gods, "you were more handsome then."

"How could my looks decline within a few hours?" said the prince. He turned to his servants.

"Did I look better in the morning?" he enquired.

"You looked the same," said his servants.

"We are gods," said one of the visitors. "We can see what your servants cannot. Their vision is imperfect and we'll prove it to you. Bring a bowl of water."

A bowl of water was brought. The god asked the servants to study it closely and then leave the room. When they were gone, he removed half a spoonful of water from the bowl.

Then the servants were called back.

"Is there any change in the bowl of water?" asked the god.

"None," said the servants.

"They cannot see that the water has diminished," said the god, "just as they cannot see that your beauty has deteriorated."

The prince was shaken. He thought, *"My beauty is*

diminishing by the day. It is short-lived. Why am I besotted by something so fleeting? I should concern myself with that which is eternal."

He never again looked into a mirror and in course of time, he renounced his throne and became a monk.

The Big Leap

Two frogs fell into a deep pit, and though they tried very hard they could not hop out.

Their comrades peered down from the top and croaked in sympathy.

"We feel for you," they shouted, "but there's no way you can get out from there!"

On hearing this, one of the frogs lost heart, and died of fear. The other frog was deaf. He thought his comrades were shouting encouragement. Emboldened by their faith in him, he gathered up all his reserves of energy into one great jump that landed him out of the pit.

Indecisiveness

A strong wind began to blow, while a washerman was washing clothes, in the shallow part of a river.

Afraid that the clothes that he had already washed and put to dry might blow away, he waded ashore to gather them up. Suddenly, he realized that his boat might break its moorings and drift. Thinking that the clothes could wait, he turned around and

began running towards his boat. Halfway there, he remembered that there were some expensive saris among the clothes that were drying. He turned around again and made a dash for the clothes. Meanwhile, the wind had gained hurricane strength. Before he could reach the clothes, they went swirling into the air. The washerman ran after them, but could not retrieve a single one.

Suddenly remembering his boat, he sprinted to the river, only to find the boat being carried away by a strong current.

Warning against such indecisiveness, the Telugu proverb says: rentiki chheda revadu – the dhobi lost both.

Foxy Fox

A tiger popped out from some bushes, frightening a shepherd, who was resting under a tree.

The shepherd picked up his staff and leaped to his feet. The tiger froze. He thought the staff was a gun.

Man and beast glared at each other, neither daring to make the first move.

Then along came a fox.

The fox took in the situation at a glance and not being one to let an opportunity slip through his paws, hit on a plan to enrich himself.

He ran up to the tiger and said, "Cousin Tiger, you're in grave danger. I'll try to persuade him not to shoot. What will you give me if I succeed?"

"Anything you ask."

The fox ran to the shepherd and said, "Uncle Shepherd, you're in grave danger. I'll try to persuade him to spare you. What will you give me if I succeed?"

"Anything you ask."

The fox ran back to the tiger.

"You're fortunate that he holds me in such high esteem," he said.

"He has agreed to spare you. Go quickly."

The tiger bounded away.

The fox went back to the shepherd.

"For all his strength, he's afraid of me," he said. "When I told him it would displease me if he attacked you, he turned pale and ran away. Now give me my reward."

"What do you want?" asked the man.

"I have not tasted flesh for days," said the fox. "Let me take a bite out of your leg."

The shepherd bared his leg and held it out to him.

"Go ahead," he said, "after all, you saved my life."

As the fox was about to bite he heard an alarming sound – the barking of dogs.

"They're mine," said the shepherd, "they follow me wherever I go. There's nothing to be afraid of."

But the fox knew there was everything to be scared of when dogs were around. Pretending to have suddenly remembered an important appointment with another tiger, he ran back into the jungle, where he knew he would be safe.

When he had got his breath back, he went in search of the tiger and found him sitting outside his den.

"Well, Cousin Tiger," he said. "I saved your life and you made a promise. Now you must keep it."

"I am no cousin to you!" growled the tiger, "and I owe you no favours. Now go before I make a meal of you!"

"There is no gratitude in the world," muttered the fox slinking away.

He saw a bear and a hunter arguing with each other. He hurried to offer them his services.

The Trouble Maker

A crabby old woman, envious of the peace and tranquility in her neighbour's house, decided to sow the seeds of discord there.

So one day, she said to the lady of the house, "Your husband is a wonderful man, but do you know he was a carrier of salt in his

last life? He carried sacks of salt on his back, from the seashore to the market place."

"How do you know?" said the young woman, annoyed, "I don't believe you. My husband is so loving and strong. He must surely have been a prince or a warrior or a poet in his past life."

"There's a sure test," said the crafty woman. "One night while he's asleep lick his back. You'll find that it's salty."

That made the young woman very angry and she walked away without another word.

The next day, the old woman waylaid the husband and said to him, "Your wife is a wonderful woman. But do you know she was a dog in her past life?"

"How do you know?" said the man, offended. "She's so gentle and loving. She must surely have been a princess in her past life."

"One of these days she'll lick your back and then you'll know I was telling the truth," said the old woman. "We are often betrayed by our actions."

The man was very angry and walked away without another word.

He did not say anything to his wife for fear of hurting her feelings, and for the same reason she did not tell him what the old woman had said about him. But one very warm night, when her husband was sleeping with his back turned to her, she was overwhelmed by a desire to find out if what the old woman had said was true and snuggling up to him gently licked his back. To her dismay, she found that it did have a salty taste.

"So it's true," she murmured. "I'm married to a man, who carried salt for a living in his past life."

Her husband, who had awakened the moment she had started licking him and had frozen in horror, now turned around, his eyes blazing.

"I may well have been a salt carrier," he said, "But do you know who you were? You were a dog! A miserable, flea-bitten dog!"

"How dare you call me a dog!" shouted his wife and launched a spirited verbal attack on his shortcomings.

The sound of the quarrel awoke their neighbour. But she didn't mind at all. In fact, she was quite pleased. Her plan had succeeded better than she had expected!

The Overconfident Fox

A fox and a wildcat met on the outskirts of a village. "This is a dangerous place," said the cat, "infested with dogs."

"Dogs don't bother me," boasted the fox. "I know a hundred ways to get away from those stupid animals."

Just then, they saw a pack of dogs coming.

"Good bye, friend," said the cat. "I'd better be going. Unlike

you, I know only one way to get away from dogs and that is to climb up a tree."

And with that it sped up a tall tree.

The fox tried all the tricks it knew in its attempt to get away from the dogs, but was soon caught.

An Uphill Task

Sisyphus of Greek mythology was a trickster, who fooled even the gods.

Towards the end of his life, he captured Thanatos, the god of death and bound him in chains, thereby bringing the process of death on earth to a halt. Normalcy returned, when the god Ares rescued Thanatos and gave him power over Sisyphus.

Then Sisyphus made ready to journey to the world of the dead. He instructed his wife not to perform any of the customary rituals, at his funeral service. He then lay down and died.

Respecting his wishes, his wife did not even bury his body. When Sisyphus arrived in Hades, he began to complain bitterly about his wife's negligence in performing the burial rites and begged to be allowed to return to earth, to set matters right. He promised to return as soon as the rituals were completed. Hades, ruler of the underworld let him go, but soon regretted his generosity, because once he was back in the land of the living, Sisyphus showed no inclination of returning to Hades.

Finally, the god Hermes succeeded in capturing him and bundled him back to the Underworld.

Sisyphus was punished for his trickery in the Underworld. He was made to roll a stone up a hill. As soon as he neared the top, the stone would slip out of his hands and roll down to the bottom and Sisyphus had to begin all over again. It was a never-ending and fruitless task.

Poor Sisyphus got nothing for it, but it has given us the word 'Sisyphean'.

Force of Habit

One day, a man found a book in his attic. As he turned
the pages of the book, he noticed that the book was so
old that the papers were yellow and some of the pages crumbled.

He discovered that it was a book on magic, but try as he
might, he could not understand any portion of it, except one
paragraph. The paragraph stated that on the shores of the Black
Sea, there was a pebble that could turn anything into gold. This
pebble, the ancient writer said, could be distinguished from the

others only by touching – unlike the other pebbles, it was warm to the touch.

The man went to the shores of the Black Sea and began to search for the pebble.

From morning to night, he would pick up pebbles and feel them. To ensure that he did not pick up the same pebble twice, he would fling every pebble he picked up far out into the sea.

The days stretched into weeks and then into months. A year passed; then another. The man went on looking for the pebble. But every pebble, he picked up was as cold as ice and he flung them away, as fast as he picked them. Now, he had become so good at it that he could pick up a pebble and fling it into the sea with one smooth action.

One evening, as he was wearily leaving the beach, when he saw a pebble in front of him.

He picked it up. It was warm. But out of force of habit he flung it far out into the sea!

A Man's True Worth

Fariduddin Attar, the chemist, was sitting in his shop, when a beggar appeared at the door and began looking at the costly perfumes kept for sale there.

"Be gone!" shouted Fariduddin.

"I'll be gone in an instant," said the beggar. "I have nothing but the clothes on my back and going away is no problem for me. You should think about yourself. Can you leave at a moment's notice like me?"

After he had gone, Fariduddin realized that what the man had said was right. His business kept him tied down and he had no real freedom. He gave away his shop to a relative and became a wanderer and a seeker of knowledge. In time, he became a great teacher, renowned for his learning and wisdom.

When he was 110 years old, the Mongols over ran Persia. He was about to be slain by a soldier, when a merchant recognized him and offered the soldier a large ransom for his life.

But Fariduddin advised the soldier not to sell him.

"The price he is offering does not represent my true worth," he told the soldier.

Another merchant offered a still larger ransom, but again, Fariduddin advised the soldier not to sell him. Then, the soldier took him to a very rich man.

"How much will you give me for this scholar?" he asked.

"A handful of straw," said the merchant.

"Sell me to him," said Fariduddin to the soldier. "That is my real worth."

The soldier was so enraged that he slew him on the spot.

Sign Language

The fish shop had changed hands and the new owner put up a signboard which read:

'Fresh Fish Sold Here'.

One day, a villager took the owner of the shop aside and advised him to remove the word 'Fresh'.

"The word is superfluous," said the man. "No one would sell fish that was stale, you know?"

So the owner deleted the word 'Fresh'.

Sometime later, another man advised him to remove the word 'Sold'.

"It is superfluous," said the man, "everyone knows you're selling the fish, not giving it away."

So the man deleted the word. A few days later, a third man advised him to remove the word 'Here'.

"Everyone knows the fish is here," said the man, "it can't be anywhere else."

So the man deleted the word 'Here'. Now, there was only one word left: 'Fish'.

"No one could possibly find fault with it now," thought the owner. But he was wrong.

One day a schoolgirl said to him, "Why have you put up that sign, sir? Everyone passing by can smell the fish. The word is entirely super... super..."

"Superfluous?" asked the man, and pulling out the signboard, flung it away.

Five Men in a Cart

Guru Gampar had told his four disciples that they were never to do anything without his permission.

One day, while they were on their way to a distant town, Guru Gampar fell asleep in the bullock cart they were travelling in. His head rolled from side-to-side and suddenly his turban slipped from his head and fell on to the road. But as their guru had told them never to do anything without his permission, none of the disciples made a move to get down and pick it up. When the guru woke up and was told about the loss of his turban, he was furious.

"Next time anything falls off, pick it up at once!" he thundered. Sometime later, the bullock dropped its dung and the four foolish disciples leaped down and picked it up. Guru Gampar was horrified. He made a list of the things that could fall off from a moving cart. "Pick up any of these things if they fall," he told them, handing them the list. "Don't pick up anything that is not mentioned here."

Just then, the cart lurched violently and Guru Gampar was thrown headlong into a ditch.

Guru Gampar yelled to his disciples to pull him out.

"We can't, Guruji," said his disciples, sadly. "Your name is not on the list you gave us." Guru Gampar pleaded with them to pull him out, but in vain.

"We know you are testing us, Guruji," they told him. "But you can rest assured that we will never disobey you. You told us not to pick up anything that was not mentioned in your list and we will not do so."

"Give me the list!" yelled Guru Gampar. They threw him the list and the pen and the guru hastily scrawled his name on it. Then and only then did the obedient disciples pull their beloved guru out of the ditch and put him back into the cart!

Leopard by the Tail

A wily merchant was crossing a short stretch of forest on foot, when he was accosted by a hungry leopard. The leopard lunged, but the merchant dodged round a tree and caught hold of its tail. Man and beast began to go round and round the tree, the man holding on to the tail for dear life. In the process, a money belt that he had tied around his waist, burst open, spilling its contents.

As the merchant was wondering what he should do next, he saw another traveller peering fearfully at him and the leopard from a safe distance. He looked ready to run.

"Don't be afraid!" he shouted to the traveller. "This is a magic leopard. If you hold its tail and run, it drops money. See how much money it has dropped for me. It's struggling to get away. Would you like to take over from me or should I let it go?"

"No, no," said the traveller, running forward. "Don't let it go! Let me make some money too!"

He ran alongside the merchant, and caught hold of the leopard's tail, whereupon the merchant quickly jumped out of the way. As soon as he had recovered his breath, the merchant

gathered up his money, and ran, paying no heed to the cries of the traveller, who had realized to his horror that, far from trying to get away, the leopard was in fact, trying to get him.

The story has been condensed in the Malayalam phrase, *Nayaru pidicha pulivaalu,* 'the leopard's tail that a Nair caught' to describe the plight of someone, who is caught in a messy situation from which he cannot easily extricate himself.

Two of a Kind

A man got into the first class compartment of a train in Belgrade, and lit a cigarette.

"You can't smoke here," said a man sitting opposite him. "This is a non-smoking compartment." But the smoker ignored him and continued smoking. Enraged, the other man leaned

out of the window and called a conductor, who was standing on the platform.

"What's the problem?" asked the conductor, coming in.

"He's smoking," said the man who had called him, jerking his head in the direction of the smoker.

"In fact, it is he who is breaking the rules," said the smoker, "he does not belong here. He has a second-class ticket."

At this, the other man turned pale. He hastily gathered up his belongings and left the compartment.

They met again by chance at the end of the journey.

"Tell me," said the non-smoker, "how did you know I had a second-class ticket? Are you a mind-reader or something?"

"Nothing of that sort," said the smoker, chuckling. "A corner of your ticket was sticking out from your pocket and I saw that it was the same colour as mine."

What Was That Sound?

A man driving through the countryside found himself outside a monastery, at sundown and decided to spend the night there.

The monks were very hospitable. They gave him supper and provided him with a comfortable bed.

He woke up with a start towards midnight. Something had awakened him. As he was wondering what it was, he heard a low, but eerie sound that sent a shudder up his spine. It stopped after some time.

The next morning, he asked the monks what the sound was, but they looked at each other and shook their heads.

"We can't tell you," they said. "You're not a monk."

The man bid them farewell and left. Some years later, by a strange coincidence, he again found himself outside the same monastery, at sundown and again, sought the hospitality of the monks. They put him up in the same bedroom in which he had spent the night on his previous visit. He found it hard to sleep, wondering if he would hear the sound that had puzzled him so much the last time. And towards midnight, he did indeed hear

it – a low ethereal sound that made his hair stand on end. The next morning, he pleaded with the monks to tell him what the sound was, but they obstinately refused.

"You're not a monk," they said, "... you're not a monk."

"I'll have no peace of mind until I know what that sound is!" said the man. "If the only way to find out is to become a monk, I'll become one! Tell me how to go about it."

"Give away your car and your fine clothes and your valuables and come back to us," said the abbot, the head of the monastery. The man gave away everything he had to the people in a nearby village and returned in his underwear. The monks gave him a robe.

"Now you're one of us," they said.

"Good," said the man. "Now tell me what that strange sound was! Who or what is making that sound?"

In answer, the abbot pointed to a door at the end of a corridor.

"Go through it and you'll find the answer," he said.

The man pushed open the door and found himself confronted by another one made of stone. He pushed open the stone door and found another one made of jade. He pushed open the jade door and found another one made of silver. He pushed open the silver door and there in front of him was the source of the sound. He was horrified. He wanted to turn and run away, but fear rooted him to the spot.

What was it that he had seen? What was the source of the mysterious sound?

Alas, dear reader, the answer cannot be revealed to you.

You're not a monk!

Tell-tale Shadow

A thief entered a temple to evade the police, and attached himself to a group of devotees there.

Somebody was singing a hymn and though the thief was not paying attention, one line from it registered in his mind and he found himself repeating it over and over again. The line was: *Gods and goddesses cast no shadow.*

When he left the temple, he was spotted by the police and arrested. The police tried to make him confess to his crime, but without success. He steadfastly maintained his innocence. The police decided to trick him into confessing. They dressed a woman as a goddess and slipped her into his cell, when he was asleep.

The thief was startled, when she shook him awake.

"Who are you?" he gasped.

"Can't you see," smiled the woman. "O mortal, confess your sins, and I will take you out of here with my divine powers."

The thief, awed by his visitor, was about to come clean, when he suddenly recalled the line he had heard in the temple:

Gods and goddesses cast no shadow.

He could clearly see his visitor's shadow on the wall.

Realizing that it was a trap, he decided to turn it around to his advantage.

"I'm innocent," he said, falling at her feet.

"Save me. I've been wrongly accused."

The woman pushed open the door of the cell, and left, promising to return in a short while.

Instead, she went directly to the chief of police and gave an account of all that had happened in the cell.

"He's certainly innocent," she opined.

"He believed I was a goddess, so he would not have dared to lie."

The thief was released. He went directly to the temple to give thanks.

He found the atmosphere there so peaceful that he became a regular temple-goer.

In course of time, he became a god-fearing person, and gave up his evil ways.

The Miserly Beggar

The king was to pass by a beggar's hut.

The man was beside himself with excitement. This was not because he was about to see the king, but because the king was known to part with expensive jewels and huge sums of money, when moved by compassion.

He saw the king's chariot, just as a kindly man was filling his begging bowl with uncooked rice. Pushing the man aside, he ran into the street, shouting praises of the king and the royal family.

The chariot stopped and the king beckoned to the beggar.

"Who are you?" he asked.

"One of the most unfortunate of your subjects," said the beggar. "Poverty sits on my doorstep and follows me about like a dog. I haven't eaten since yesterday afternoon!"

"Have you nothing for your king except a tale of woe?" said the ruler, putting out his hand. "Give me something."

The beggar, astonished, carefully picked up five grains of rice from his bowl and laid them on the king's outstretched palm.

The king drove away. The beggar's disappointment was great. He raved and ranted and cursed the king again and again for

his miserliness. Finally, his anger spent, he went on his rounds.

When he returned home in the evening, he found a bag of rice on the floor.

"Some generous soul has been here," he thought and took out a handful of rice from the bag. To his astonishment, there was a small piece of gold in it. He realized then that the bag had been sent by the king. He emptied the rice on the floor, feeling sure there would be more gold pieces in it, and he was right. He found five, one for each grain of rice he had given the king.

"It is not the king who has been miserly," thought the man, sadly.

"If I had been generous and given him the whole bowl of rice, I would have been a rich man today."

Tales of Wit and Wisdom

A Hundred Faces

A king riding through the countryside met a peasant. Being ever concerned about the welfare of his subjects, he asked him how much he earned.

"Four coins each day, your majesty," replied the man.

"And how do you spend the four coins?"

"One on myself, one I give in gratitude, one I give back and one I give on interest."

The king, puzzled, asked him to explain.

"A part of the money I spend on myself," said the man, "a part on my wife in gratitude for all she does for the house, a part on my aged parents to pay them back for all that they did for me and a part on my children, who I expect will pay me back with interest, by looking after me and my wife in our old age."

"You have provided me a fine riddle," said the king. "Please keep the answer a secret for some time, at least until you've seen my face a hundred times."

"I will," said the peasant.

That very evening, the king put the riddle to his courtiers. He related to them, the peasant's answer in response to his question about how he spent his money and asked them to explain what the peasant had meant. The courtiers could not think of a proper reply, but one of them said he would have the answer in twenty-four hours.

He sought out the peasant and asked him the answer to the riddle. The man, at first, refused to reveal the answer, but was eventually persuaded to do so with a gift of a bag of coins. When the courtier returned to the palace and told the king the answer to the riddle, the monarch guessed that the peasant had broken his promise of silence.

He sent for the man and asked him why he had betrayed his trust.

"Didn't I tell you not to reveal the answer until you had seen my face a hundred times?" demanded the king.

"But I did see your face a hundred times, before I told him the answer, your majesty," replied the peasant. "He gave me a bag of hundred coins and each of them had your face on it."

The king was delighted with his wit and rewarded him handsomely.

Battle of Wits

Subuddhi and Kubuddhi were always trying to get the better of each other.

One day, in October, Kubuddhi saw a mango growing on his tree. He knocked it down, wrapped it in a cloth and waited for Subuddhi to come by.

When he did, he called out to him. "I have a riddle for you," he said. "Can you tell me what fruit is wrapped in this cloth? If you guess correctly, you may take any one thing from my house that you can carry out with your two hands; if you fail, I'll come to your house and carry away something."

"All right," said Subuddhi, always ready to match his wits with Kubuddhi. "It must be a guava."

"No," said the other man. "I'll give you two more guesses."

"It is the season for custard apples," said Subuddhi. "It must be a custard apple."

"Last guess."

"Pomegranate?"

"You've failed," said Kubuddhi and triumphantly uncovered the mango.

"I'll go home and prepare for your visit," said Subuddhi. "Come in half an hour."

Thirty minutes later, Kubuddhi was at the gates of Subuddhi's house.

A glint of metal caught his eye and looking up; he saw there was a chest on the roof.

"Tell me truthfully," he said to Subuddhi, "does that chest contain anything valuable?"

"Yes," said Subuddhi, "all my money and most of my wife's ornaments. I thought I had concealed it well."

"You should've covered it," said Kubuddhi, gleefully. "Now though it is outside your house, it is still part of your house and I can claim it."

"You have to lay your hands on it first. Remember, you may take only one thing from my house."

"One is enough," said Kubuddhi. He went boldly into Subuddhi's house, brought out a ladder and placed it against the roof.

"Yes, kindly take it down for me," said Subuddhi, "and I must thank you for sparing my valuables."

"Sparing your valuables?" said Kubuddhi, perplexed. "What makes you think I'm going to let you keep your valuables?"

"We had agreed you could take away one thing that you could carry out with your own two hands," said Subuddhi, grinning. "And you have carried out the ladder."

Tug of War

There was a rabbit that enjoyed playing tricks on other animals.

One day, as he was walking in the woods near the sea, he came across a huge elephant pulling out and eating leaves from a tree.

"How are you, Mr. Elephant?" he called out. "My, how much you eat!"

"That's because I'm so big," replied the elephant. "Small animals like you don't need much food, but large and powerful animals like me need a lot!"

"Large you certainly are!" said the rabbit, "but powerful…?"

"You don't think I'm powerful?" asked the elephant, sounding surprised, and also a little annoyed.

"I'm sure you are," said the rabbit, "but are you more powerful than me?"

The elephant thought he had not heard right.

"Powerful? You?"

"Yes, me."

The elephant doubled up with laughter.

"You're laughing because you don't know how strong I am," said the rabbit. "If you let me tie a rope around your middle, I'll drag you into the sea."

"Drag me into the sea?" laughed the elephant. "Hoo-hooo – hoooo! Well, go ahead! Tie a rope around me and let me see how far you can pull me!"

The rabbit tied a thick rope around the elephant's body.

"When you feel a tug on the rope, be ready to pull," he said, "or you'll be dragged into the sea, before you know what's happening!"

"Please don't pull too hard," mocked the elephant.

The rabbit ran to the seashore with the other end of the rope.

He saw a whale swimming some distance away, and called out to it. When the whale drew near, he said, "Mr. Whale you're so big, but are you strong?"

"I'm the strongest animal on Earth!" bellowed the whale.

"I'll show you how wrong you are," said the rabbit. "Let me tie this rope around your middle."

"And then?"

"I'll drag you ashore."

The whale doubled up with laughter.

"All right, go ahead," he giggled. "Tie your rope around me and pull me out!"

The rabbit tied the rope securely around the whale's middle. Then he ran ashore and rushing into the woods, hid behind a tree and shouted, "PULL!"

The elephant, intending to throw the rabbit high into the sky to frighten him, wrapped his trunk around the rope and gave a mighty heave upwards. The whale countered with a tug that almost brought the elephant to his knees. The two animals, hidden from each other's sight by the trees in between, marvelled at the strength of the rabbit. They pulled and heaved and exerted their strength to the utmost, but neither could get the better of the other. Finally, the rope broke and the two animals fled in opposite directions.

From then on, whenever the elephant saw the rabbit, he would quickly hide himself or run away, to the great amusement of the rabbit.

Heads or Tails?

The king's men were uneasy. They were on their way to put down a rebellion, led by a ruthless and ferocious chieftain, but they were no match for the rebel's forces.

Their commander, a grizzled veteran of many campaigns, knew that unless he could boost their morale, the battle was as good as lost. There was a temple nearby. He told the soldiers he would go in and pray for guidance. When he came out some time later, he looked dazed.

"I heard a voice," he told his men. "The voice has asked me

to toss a coin. If it shows heads we will win. If it shows tails, we will lose."

He took out a coin and tossed it. It landed to show heads. He tossed it twice more and each time it showed heads.

"This is a sure sign of victory," said the soldiers.

They charged ferociously at the opposing army and routed it.

They returned home to a glorious welcome.

The commander's grandson ran forward and hugged him. "What have you brought for me, grandfather?" he asked.

"This," said the commander, giving him the coin he had tossed up in front of his men.

"Keep it carefully. It is not an ordinary coin. See, it has heads on both sides.

Murugan Raises the Alarm

One night, Murugan was woken up by his wife. Hearing a noise in the kitchen, she feared that a thief had got in.

Murugan felt that if he raised an alarm, the thief would attack him. So he thought of a plan and

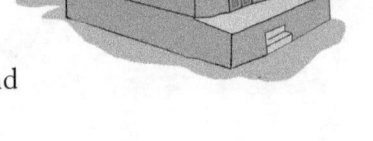

whispered it into his wife's ear.

The thief, who was trying to find out whether Murugan and his wife were asleep, suddenly heard Murugan's wife speaking.

"But what if the child is a boy?" he heard her say. "What shall we name him then?"

"If our child is a boy, we'll name him Varada," said Murugan.

"Why Varada?" asked his wife.

"It's so easy to pronounce," said Murugan. "If he's near, you can call softly, 'Varada, Varada.' If he's at a distance you can call louder, 'Varada' and if he's far away you can shout 'VARADA! VARADA'. And he began to shout out the name.

Now Varada was the name of the local Kotwal, the Chief of Police. He was patrolling the streets and when he heard his name being called, he rushed into Murugan's house. Finding that a window had been forced open, he entered through it and nabbed the thief, who was cowering behind the kitchen door.

The next day, the people of the village marvelled at the way Murugan had raised the alarm, without arousing the thief's suspicion.

Body Chart

I t was a sweltering hot day in summer.

The village school teacher, dripping with sweat could bear it no longer. He put down the book from which he was reading, removed his shirt and hung it on a nail beside the blackboard.

Instantly, he felt better.

But just as he was about to pick up the book again, a student, whose eyes were always on the road outside made a choking sound.

"What is it?" asked the school teacher, impatiently.

"The… I… Inspector, sir!" gasped the boy, his eyes rolling in alarm. "…The Inspector is coming!"

The teacher was petrified. Out of the corner of his eye, he saw the door opening. It was too late to lunge for his shirt. . .

Then suddenly, he knew what to do. "And so, children," he said, "do you now know where the lungs are situated in the body? Look again, See here. . ." and he tapped his thin, bony chest.

"What is going on?" asked the Inspector behind him.

The teacher whirled round in mock alarm.

"Do you mean to say," continued the Inspector, "that you don't have a chart showing the positions of the organs of the body?"

"Alas, sir, no," said the teacher, hastily pulling on his shirt. "So many times I have written to the department but. . ."

"Oh, you poor man!" said the Inspector, "I will see to it that you get the charts at once!"

Moreover, he got them too – along with an increment of rupees fifteen in his salary.

The inspector touched by his dedication to his duty had recommended it!

The Challenge

Tales of the witty Gopal Bhand are popular in Bengal.

One day, Gopal bought a large hilsa fish and was taking it home, when he met the local zamindar.

"That's a fine fish you've got there," said the zamindar. "How much did you pay for it?"

Gopal told him.

"You'd better keep shouting the price as you go along," said the zamindar. "Everybody you meet is going to ask you about it!"

"That's true," said Gopal.

"They say, you're very clever," continued the zamindar. "Let me test your cleverness. I challenge you to take that fish all the way to your house, in full view of everybody, without anybody asking you how much you paid for it!"

Gopal accepted the challenge.

Sometime later, people walking on the road leading to Gopal's house were astonished to see a near-naked man, daubed in mud, carrying a large fish on his head, who was walking

towards them. On closer scrutiny, they saw it was Gopal. They asked him what had happened to him and why he was covered in mud. But Gopal did not answer.

Only when he reached home and the door had closed behind him that, he opened his mouth – to laugh.

He had succeeded in bringing the fish home, without anybody asking its price!

When the zamindar heard how cleverly Gopal had diverted people's attention from the fish, he was filled with admiration and rewarded him handsomely.

Raman Advises an Artist

Tenali Raman was a jester, at the court of King Krishnadevaraya of Vijayanagar. Many stories are told about his wit and wisdom. Here is one such story...

An artist was commissioned to make a portrait of a certain prince. The artist drew a fine picture, but the prince did not like it.

"It does not resemble me at all!" he said and sent the artist away, without paying him.

The artist sought Tenali Rama's help and following his advice nailed the picture to a tree outside the palace. On the picture, again on Rama's advice, he wrote the word, 'Fool'.

The prince was very angry, when he saw the picture. He had the artist brought before him.

"How dare you call me a fool!?" thundered the prince.

"I would never do such a thing, Your Highness," said the artist. "The picture on the tree does not represent you. You, yourself told me that it does not resemble you."

The prince realized he had been unjust to the artist. He accepted the painting and paid the artist twice the amount he had contracted to pay him.

Raman's List of Fools

One day a horse trader, a foreigner, came to the court
of Krishnadeva Raya and told him he had some fine
horses for sale. The emperor offered to buy them. The man took

an advance of 5000 gold coins and promising to return with the horses in two days, went away. That evening, Krishnadeva Raya saw Raman writing on a sheet of paper.

"What are you writing?" he asked.

"I'm making a list of the greatest fools in the empire," said Raman.

The emperor was astonished to see his own name on the top of the list.

"What is the meaning of this?" he demanded. "You think I am a fool!"

"Any man who gives 5000 gold coins to a stranger and expects him to return them, is a fool," replied Raman.

"Oh, so that's what is troubling you," said the emperor. "You think the man won't return. What if he does?"

"In that case," said Raman with a twinkle in his eye, "I'll scratch out your name and put his there."

The Demon's Share

One day, a demon came to see a farmer, who was working in his field.

"These fields belonged to my father's father," said the demon, "I will take half of whatever you grow in these fields."

The farmer was frightened, but he kept his wits about him.

"You can take whatever grows above the ground, your Excellency," he said.

The demon agreed and went away.

That year the farmer grew potatoes in his field. When the demon came for his share, he got the stems and leaves of the plant, but not a single potato, since it grows underground.

"Next time, I'll take whatever grows under the ground!" he growled.

When he came again some months later, the farmer was harvesting corn. He had planted wheat and had got a bumper harvest. "Where's my share?" screamed the demon.

"Your share is under the ground, your Excellency," said the farmer. You can take the roots away whenever you want."

The demon, ashamed at being outwitted by a farmer, turned around without another word and walked away.

The farmer never saw him again.

The Three Pots

A rich landowner was on his deathbed. Gasping for breath, he told his three sons to dig under his bed when he was gone, and saying that, gave up the ghost.

Some days later, the sons dug at the spot and unearthed three pots, placed one above the other. The topmost pot contained mud; the middle pot contained dried cow dung, and the lowest pot contained straw. Below this pot there was a silver coin.

The brothers were perplexed.

"Obviously, father meant to convey some message to us

through the pots and their contents," said the oldest brother. "But what?"

They wracked their brains, but none of them could come up with an explanation. Finally, they decided to consult their doctor, who was also a family friend.

The doctor laughed, when the brothers put their problem before him.

"Your father loved puzzles," he said, "and I think he could not resist setting one last one. The interpretation is simple. The topmost pot contains mud, you say. That means he wants his eldest son to have his fields. The second pot contains cow dung. It means he wants his second son to have his herd of cattle. The last pot contains straw. Now straw is golden-coloured. That means he wants his youngest son to have all his gold."

The brothers were happy with the way their father had apportioned his wealth and marvelled at the doctor's sagacity.

"But one thing remains unexplained," said the youngest brother, "the silver coin at the bottom of the pots."

"Your father knew you would come to consult me," smiled the doctor. "The coin is my fee."

Birbal Shortens a Road

The emperor Akbar was travelling to a distant place along with some of his courtiers.

It was a hot day and the emperor was tiring of the journey.

"Can't anybody shorten this road for me?" he asked, querulously.

"I can," said Birbal.

The other courtiers looked at one another, perplexed. All of them knew there was no other path through the hilly terrain. The road they were travelling on was the only one that, could take them to their destination.

"You can shorten the road?" said the emperor. "Well, do it."

"I will," said Birbal. "First, listen to this story I have to tell."

Then riding beside the emperor's palanquin, he launched upon a long and intriguing tale that held Akbar and all those listening, spellbound. Before they knew it, they had reached the end of their journey.

"We've reached?" exclaimed Akbar. "So soon!"

"Well," grinned Birbal, "you did say that you wanted the road to be shortened."

The Witness

A trader borrowed a large sum of money from a moneylender and despite repeated reminders failed to repay it. One day the money lender went to the trader's house, when he was entertaining guests and demanded the money. The embarrassed trader promised to come to his place the next day with the money. But he had no intention of repaying the loan. Instead, he wanted to take revenge against the moneylender for humiliating him in front of his guests.

So one evening, he waylaid the man on a deserted stretch of road. "No one can insult me and get away with it!" he said, drawing out his sword.

The money lender thought fast. "I was expecting you would do something like this," he said. "I've left a letter with my wife. If I do not return home by nightfall, she will take the letter to the king. The letter details the business transaction between us and the steps I took to recover the money. It also expresses the fear that you might do me some harm."

The trader lowered his sword. He knew that the money lender could be bluffing, but he did not want to take a chance. The king was known to be harsh on defaulters and murderers.

"I'll spare your worthless life," he said, finally, "but I'll chop off your nose. That'll teach you a lesson you'll never forget."

"If I write off your loan, will you forgive me?" asked the money lender.

"I might," said the trader, guardedly, "but you must give me a receipt to say I've paid you in full. I don't trust you."

"I'll make a receipt right away," said the money lender, hastily opening his bundle of books. "But we'll require a witness."

"No witness!" cried the trader. "Just give me a receipt to say that I've paid you in full."

"The receipt has no value unless there is a witness," said

the money lender. "Why don't we make that old banyan tree a witness?"

The trader reasoned that there could be no harm in making the banyan tree a witness. It could not reveal the circumstances in which the receipt was made. So he agreed. They stood under the banyan tree and the money lender wrote out the receipt and gave it to the trader, who pocketed it and went away, feeling very pleased with himself.

But the very next day, he received a summons from the king. When he went to the king's palace he found the money lender there.

"Did you borrow money from this man?" asked the king.

"I did," said the trader.

"Why haven't you repaid it?"

"But I have," said the trader and triumphantly taking out the receipt from his pocket, and handed it over to the king.

"So your witness was a banyan tree," said the king, looking at the receipt.

"Yes," said the trader, "there was nobody else there."

"So you admit accosting him in a deserted spot?"

"No, no," said the trader, panicking. "I...I... just happened to meet him there."

"Anyway this receipt is useless," said the king. "It does not carry this man's signature, only that of the witness."

"What!" gasped the trader, taking the paper from the king's hand.

He stared at it and turned pale. Instead of putting his signature at the bottom, the money lender had scribbled: 'Banyan Tree'.

No Witnesses

A man's house had been burgled.

A few days later, the man was walking down the street in another part of the town, when he happened to look into a house and saw a pot, which he at once recognized as his own. He went in and there he found all the articles that were stolen from his house.

He took the owner of the house to court. The judge was a crusty old man.

"Did you see him taking the things from your house?" he asked the complainant.

"No," said the man.

"Did anyone see him taking things from your house? Can you produce any witnesses?"

"No," said the man.

"In that case I cannot convict him," said the judge. "There is no proof that he stole anything from your house."

The complainant did not say anything, but he took off one of his slippers and began belabouring the man with it.

"What are you doing!" shouted the judge.

"I am beating him because he did not inform me of his intention to rob my house," said the man. "I would have kept people to observe him doing it."

The Servant's Ruse

A man was expecting a visit from an acquaintance. He gave two ripe mangoes to his servant and asked him to slice them and serve the fruit, when the man came.

The servant gave in to temptation and ate a slice. It was so sweet that he could not resist eating another one. Then the madness of gluttony seized him and he devoured all the remaining pieces.

Suddenly, he saw the man his master was expecting coming towards the house. He thought fast. He grabbed a rusty knife and rushing to his master told him that he couldn't cut the mangoes as the knife was blunt.

"I'll sharpen it," said his master. Going to a stone in the garden, he began to rub the cutting edge of the knife against it.

Leaving him to the task, the servant ran out to meet the man who was coming.

"Beware! Beware!" he said, when he reached him. "Don't come to our house. My master has gone mad. He's planning to cut off both your ears."

"Cut off my ears!" exclaimed the man, turning pale. "Why?"

"There he is sharpening the knife," said the servant. The man saw that his host did indeed have a knife in his hands, and was sharpening it with what looked to him like a maniacal fury. He did not wait to find out why his host wanted his ears. He turned around and started walking away as fast as he could.

The servant rushed back to his master and told him that the man he had invited was running away with the mangoes.

"What!" said his master. "The greedy fellow! Has he taken both the mangoes?"

"Yes," said the servant.

The man ran after the acquaintance shouting:

"Give me one! Give me one at least!"

The other man thought that he was asking for one of his ears and ran for his life!

One Up

A man with one eye said to his friend, "I bet I can see more with my one eye than you can with your two." His friend accepted the bet.

"I've won!" said the one-eyed man. "I can see two eyes in your face whereas you can see only one in mine!"

The Poet's Reward

The poet Abu Dalameh wrote a poem in praise of the king, and the monarch, pleased, asked him what he would like as a reward.

"Give me a hound," said the poet. The courtiers looked at each other in disbelief. They felt the poet had missed a golden opportunity to make some money and pitied him.

"If it is a hound you want, you've got it," said the king.

"Your Majesty is generous," said the poet. "Now if I had a horse I could go hunting with the hound."

"You can have a horse too," said the king.

The poet said, "When I return from the hunt, it would be nice if I had someone to cook the game I have brought."

The king gave him a cook.

"Your generosity is boundless," said the poet. "But where will I keep all these presents, you have heaped on me?"

The king gave him a mansion.

"I am overwhelmed," said the poet. "But how will I maintain such a large establishment, Your Majesty?"

"I will give you a date plantation," said the king. "It will fetch you enough to run a palace."

"Never has the world known such generosity," said the poet, and kissed the king's hand and left, leaving the courtiers dumbfounded.

The Three Runners

In the days when whites ruled South Africa and apartheid was the law of the land, two middle-aged blacks met in a 'whites only' section of Johannesburg.

One of them had a permit to work in the area, the other did not, which meant he could be put behind bars for trespassing into an exclusive zone.

Suddenly, they saw a policeman coming towards them, and froze.

"Run!" whispered the man with the permit to his friend, "I'll follow."

They started running and the policeman shouting, "Stop, stop," began chasing them.

Finally, he caught the second man.

"Did you think you could outrun me!" he snarled. "Show me your permit!"

The man, playing for time, began fumbling in his pocket and finally produced his permit.

The policeman was taken aback. He realized that he had been tricked. The man without the permit was now too far away to be caught.

"When you had a permit why did you run!" he bawled.

"Doctor's orders," said the man, "he has asked me to run a mile every evening."

"Oh, yes?" sneered the policeman, "Then why was your friend running?"

"His doctor too has ordered him to run," said the man.

The policeman became red with anger.

"You think you're very smart, don't you?" he snarled. "But tell me, if you were only running for your health, why didn't you stop when you saw me running after you? And don't tell me you didn't see me chasing you... I know you did!"

"Of course, I knew you were running after me," said the man.

"Then why didn't you stop?" asked the policeman, triumphantly.

"It was stupid of me," said the man, "but I thought you too had been ordered to run by your doctor."

Holes

Moishe, the carpenter, returning home with his week's wages, was accosted by an armed robber on a deserted street.

"Take my money," said Moishe, "but do me a favour, shoot

a bullet through my hat otherwise my wife won't believe I was robbed."

The robber obliged. He threw Moishe's hat into the air and put a bullet through it.

"Let's make it look as if I ran into a gang of robbers," said Moishe, "otherwise my wife will call me a coward! Please shoot a number of holes through my coat."

So the robber shot a number of holes through the carpenter's coat.

"And now..."

"Sorry," interrupted the robber. "No more holes. I'm out of bullets."

"That's all I wanted to know!" said Moishe. "Now hand me back my money and some more for the hat and coat that you've ruined or I'll beat you black and blue!"

The robber threw down the money and ran away.

A Handful of Answers

A young student of Zen was going to the market to buy vegetables for the monastery, where he was studying.

On the way, he met a student from another monastery.

"Where are you going?" asked the first student.

"Wherever my legs take me," replied the other.

The first student pondered over the answer, as he was sure it had some deep significance. When he returned to the monastery, he reported the conversation to his teacher, who said, "You should have asked him what he would do if he had no legs."

The next day, the student was thrilled to see the same boy coming towards him.

"Where are you going?" he asked and without waiting for a reply continued, "Wherever your legs take you, I suppose. Well, let me ask you . . ."

"You're mistaken," interrupted the other boy. "Today I'm going wherever the wind blows."

This answer so confused the first boy that he could not think of anything to say.

When he reported the matter to his teacher, the old man said, "You should have asked him what he would do if there were no wind."

Some days later, the student saw the boy in the market again and rushed to confront him, confident that this time he would have the last word.

"Where are you going?" he asked. "Wherever your legs take you, or wherever the wind blows? Well, let me ask you . . . . "

"No, no," interrupted the boy. "Today I'm going to buy vegetables."

A Boaster Humbled

Antao claimed he was the biggest man in the world and was always bragging about his great strength.

One day, another giant who lived in another part of the country heard of Antao's boasts and was enraged.

"How dare he call himself the strongest man when I am here!" he roared and set out for Antao's abode.

When Antao saw him coming, he was terrified because the man was very much bigger than he was.

"What a fool I was to boast about my strength," thought Antao. "Now I'm done for!"

Suddenly, his eyes fell on an old pram, the kind that is used to wheel babies around in and he got an idea...

When the giant, who had come in search of Antao, pushed open the door of the house and entered, the first thing he saw was the pram and its occupant. It struck him that the baby was extraordinarily large. He could not see its face, but its arms and half its torso and legs hung over the sides.

"If the baby is so large," thought the giant, "its father must be a mountain of a man!"

All his courage drained from him. He turned around and fled.

People saw him running and became convinced that Antao was indeed the strongest man in the world. However, Antao himself never boasted about his strength again. He had vowed never to do so, while lying in the pram.

Crooked Howler

A thief hired a room at an inn and stayed there for a night. The next morning, when he looked out of his window, he saw the owner of the inn sitting in the courtyard. The man was

wearing an expensive new coat, which the thief decided would look good on him.

Accordingly, he went out and sitting beside the innkeeper, struck up a conversation with him. Presently, he yawned and then to the innkeeper's astonishment, howled like a wolf.

"Why did you do that?" asked the innkeeper.

"I have no control over it," said the thief. "If I yawn three times, I actually turn into a wolf. Please don't leave me. I'm frightened!" And with that he yawned again and let out another howl. The innkeeper turned pale and got up to go, but the thief caught hold of his coat and begged him to stay. Even as he pleaded, he yawned again. The terrified innkeeper wriggled out of the coat to which the thief was tightly holding on and ran into the inn and locked himself in.

The thief calmly put on the coat and walked away.

The Scholarly Coachman

Mulla Nasruddin once took up a job as a coachman and one day, he had to drive his employer to a disreputable part of the town.

"Keep your eyes open," his employer advised him, as he alighted from the coach, at his destination, "this place is infested with thieves."

Sometime later, the man thought of checking on his new employee.

"Is everything all right? What are you doing now?" he shouted, from a window of the house he had gone into.

"I'm sitting here wondering what happens to a man's lap when he gets up," the Mulla shouted back.

A little later, the employer again shouted from the window,"

"What are you doing now?"

"I'm wondering what happens to a fist when the fingers are unclenched," shouted Nasruddin.

His employer was impressed.

"My coachman is no ordinary fellow," he boasted to his hosts. "He is a philosopher!"

Half an hour later, he again poked his head out of the window and shouted!

"What are you doing now?"

"I am wondering who stole the horses," replied the Mulla.

The Fear of God

There were two brothers, who were always up to some mischief.

If somebody had been locked up in his house, or if somebody's dog had been painted green, one always knew who the culprits were – the brothers.

One day, the boys' mother asked a priest to talk to her sons and put the fear of God in them, so that they would mend their ways. The priest asked her to send her sons to him one at a time.

When the younger boy, a lad of thirteen, came, he made him sit and asked him, "Where is God?"

The boy did not answer.

The priest asked again, in a louder voice, "Where is God?"

The boy remained silent. But when the priest asked the same question a third time, the boy jumped up and ran away.

He went straight to his brother.

"We are in big trouble!" he gasped.

"What's wrong?" asked the older boy, warily, wondering which of their sins had caught up with them.

"God is missing," said the youngster, "and they think we have something to do with it!"

Cakes for the Mulla

An acquaintance barged into Nasruddin's house, one evening, hoping to be rewarded for the news he had brought.

"My neighbours are baking cakes!" he announced.

"Is that so?" said the Mulla. "How does that concern me?"

"I've heard they're going to give you some!" said the man.

"Is that so?" said the Mulla, his face brightening. "How does that concern you?"

Fired by Fear

Mulla Nasruddin was trying to raise a fire, by blowing at the glowing embers of coal in the fireplace. All he succeeded in doing was to produce a thick cloud of smoke that stung his eyes. He put on his wife's cap to prevent the smoke from getting into his eyes and started blowing again.

This time, flames leaped up from the coal.

"Ahha!" said the Mulla. "So you too are afraid of my wife."

Sweet Quarrels

One day, Mulla Nasruddin quarrelled with his wife. He shouted at her until she could not bear it and fled to her neighbour's house.

The Mulla followed her there. The neighbours managed to placate the angry husband and served the couple tea and sweetmeats.

When they returned to their house sometime later, they began quarrelling again. When Nasruddin began shouting at her, his wife again opened the door to run out.

"This time, go to the baker's house," he advised, "he makes delicious cakes."

The Noseless Mendicant

A mendicant, who had taken to dacoity was captured and brought before the king.

The punishment for dacoity was mutilation of the nose. When his nose was cut off, the mendicant began to shout, "I can see God … I can see God!"

He began to roam the countryside shouting in this way.

When people asked him why they could not see God too, he replied, "You cannot see him because your nose comes in the way. Cut off your nose and you too will see him."

One man, desperate for a vision of God cut off his nose.

"Now can you see God?" asked the mendicant.

"Yes, yes, I can," replied the man. Thereupon, several others cut off their noses too.

The cult of the Noseless Ones grew by leaps and bounds. The king heard of the cult and had the leader, the former mendicant, brought to the palace.

"Can you really see God?" asked the king.

"Yes," said the mendicant.

"If I cut off my nose will I see him too?"

"Undoubtedly."

When the man had gone, the king confided to his chief minister that his desire to see God was so great that, he would not mind joining the cult of the Noseless Ones.

The minister was aghast.

"One should not act hastily," he advised. "The eyes are situated above the nose. I cannot understand how it could obstruct one's vision. The man is a fraud."

"What about his followers?" asked the king. "They too claim they can see God."

"They do not want to admit they were fooled," said the minister. "So they too keep chanting, 'I can see God … I can see God.'"

The king was not convinced. The minister took him to the

royal prison and asked the warden to bring out a certain dacoit, who had recently been imprisoned there. When the man was brought before them, the king saw that he was noseless.

"Did your life change when your nose was cut off?" asked the king.

"Yes," said the dacoit. "I can breathe easier, now. No more do I have a stuffy nose."

"But can you see God?" asked the king.

"Yes," said the dacoit.

"You can see God?" asked the minister incredulously.

"My king is my god," said the prisoner, unctuously. "Only he can save me from this god-awful prison."

"No, no, you idiot!" shouted the king. "Can you see the real God?"

The dacoit shook his head.

The king now became convinced that the mendicant was a fraud. He was furious and sent his men to fetch him. When the man saw the soldiers coming he realized that the game was up.

"Better to be noseless than headless!" was his last message he shouted to his followers, as he fled from the back door.

He was never seen or heard of again.